Dames for Hire

HoloCity Case Files #1

S.C. Jensen

Northern Edge Publishing

First e-book edition March 2021

First print edition May 2022

ISBN 978-1-990306-11-2

Cover design by Martin — Cover Art Studio

www.coverartstudio.com

www.scjensen.com

Contents

Introduction

THANK YOU FOR PICKING up a copy of HoloCity Case Files #1: Dames for Hire!

This novella is my personal homage to the great noir pulp writer, Raymond Chandler. Here I've reimagined one of my favourites of his short stories, "Trouble is My Business" (1939), through the lens of my own hard-boiled detective, Bubbles Marlowe, in the cyberpunk setting of HoloCity.

In this story, I've repurposed some of the slang popular in American pulp novels from the 1920s – 1940s. I have tried to make meanings clear with context; however, if you need clarification on any unfamiliar words, I have provided a glossary in the back with the original meanings and how they are used in HoloCity.

If you'd like to read more about Bubbles' adventures, please check out Tropical Punch, the first book in my cyber-noir detective series, Bubbles in Space.

Enjoy!

Chapter One

I HID IN THE narrow gutter between two skyscrapers of mirrored black glass, crouched behind a dumpster that had more security features than my apartment. The tops of the towers disappeared into the yellow-grey mist of early morning smog, and the sky pissed down on me. The thin light hadn't reached the alley yet—maybe it never did. Not even the rats moved in the oppressive stillness. I held my breath and wished I hadn't come.

A door cracked open and a dark hand reached out into the rain, beckoning me inside. When I didn't move, Rae Adesina poked her blue-haired head out into the alley and blinked at me through thick, black-framed glasses. Rain dripped onto her oblong afro, and she pulled her lab coat up over her head and scowled at me.

"What's the smoke, Bubbles?" She gestured furiously, her wide, painted lips pressed into a thin line, but I shook my head.

"I can't do it." The metal fist of my left arm clenched as I pulled myself out from behind the dumpster.

Rae made a disgusted noise in the back of her throat. "You came all the way here to stand in the rain and tell me that?"

Strands of wet, pink hair fell into my eyes. I wiped them away with my flesh hand. "You didn't tell me it was an inside job."

"Come on, Bubbles." She kicked the door open all the way and stood there with her hands on her hips. "It's me."

"You saved my life, Rae. I owe you one, but—"

"You owe me more than one, girl," she said. "I put my job on the line to save your candy pink ass, and I'm calling it in now."

"This is Libra, Rae. I am not poking this bear with a ten-foot pole."

"You don't even know what I need you to do yet."

"I don't need to know. I could walk into that building, see the wrong thing, and be dead before tomorrow morning. I know you work for them—and frankly, that makes you a little scary too—but no one in their right mind ... Look. I barely survived the last time I got involved with something like this."

"You did survive. Because I saved you."

"Please don't ask me to do this."

"Fine. Give it to me."

"What?"

"Come on. Give it. You don't want to hold up your end, you can give it back."

"You want my arm?"

"Well, I can't take back your life, can I?" She snapped her fingers. "Besides, it's my arm. I made it. Give it back."

The buildings shielded me from the worst of the downpour, but the spatter built up and streamed into my eyes and down my back. My pink faux-fur jacket looked like the discarded corpse of some poor lab animal. The dumpster next to me probably had a few just like it. "Rae. You're killing me."

Rae's big dark eyes softened a little. "When's the last time you had a drink, Bubbles?"

"Before," I said. I dry-swallowed against the thirst that thickened my throat. Even her asking made my heart beat faster. "Before the accident."

"Don't call it that," Rae said, her voice a hoarse whisper. "You know it wasn't an accident."

The upgrade clenched and unclenched against my thigh. It didn't always do what I wanted it to. The amputation was fresh. The nerves hadn't healed all the way. Rae had taught me how to use it, but I still wasn't used to it.

"I'm sorry, Rae." Hot tears stung my eyes and I was grateful for the rain and the dark. I didn't want her to see me like this. Weak and scared and dying for a drink. The cold and the wet caught up to me suddenly. I wrapped my arms around my body to stop the shaking. It didn't help. "I just ... I don't know what I'm doing."

"I get it. You're terrified. You should be," Rae said. "But not of me. This. I'm trying to help you."

"I'm retired." I laughed bitterly and stared into the depths of an oily black puddle. "Chief Swain didn't kill me, but he ended me just the same. I can't get involved with the HCPD. I promised."

"That's exactly why Flint wants to see you."

My gaze snapped back to Rae's face. "Flint? As in Wallace Flint, your boss?"

"That's the one." Behind the black-rimmed glasses, her dark eyes watched me carefully.

"You hate that guy."

"How I feel about him has nothing to do with it." Rae sighed impatiently. "The fact is, he has a personal problem, and I suggested he talk to you about it. You can help him. He can help you. You helping him, helps me. Get it?"

"It's not Swain's turf?"

"No. And Flint wants to keep it that way. He's being headhunted by one of the Trade Zone's private R&D teams, and he can't afford any blemishes on his record. He only talked to me because—"

"Because you get his job when he leaves," I said. "You'll protect him."

Rae tossed her hands into the air and tipped her head to the thick stew of smog above us. "She sees the light!"

I kicked the surface of the puddle and watch the iridescent ripples settle. I still didn't want to do it. I'd only been retired from the HCPD for a couple weeks. The fear and the pain were still fresh, carved into bas relief by the hard edge of sobriety. Swain had already taken my arm and my job. He'd tried to take my life. I wasn't a red smear on the pavement like he'd intended, but I might as well have been. Without the job, I was nothing.

Just a Grit District skid with an upgrade I couldn't afford and a habit that might kill me to break.

So what did I have to lose?

I groaned and heaved myself reluctantly up the steps toward the yawning black hole into the glittering obsidian tower. "This is the stupidest thing I've ever done."

"No it isn't." Rae grinned at me with huge white teeth. "Not even close. Remember that time you drank thirteen ruby gimlets, tried to make out with a HoloPop ad for Big Al's Waste Disposal, and then puked in my best Cosmo Régale handbag?"

"No."

She turned and walked into the dark corridor beyond the door. "You still owe a new bag."

"Don't remind me." The door slammed shut behind me. The sound of grinding electronic mechanisms echoed in the darkness as the door ensured I would never be able to leave of my own volition. "What exactly is this job?"

"Put these on." Rae shoved a pair of glasses on my face and checked the fitting. They sat snug over my cheeks and forehead, like a diving mask. Once they were in place, she pushed a button on the side and bright green lines lit up along the floor. "You'll be able to see enough to walk with these, but not enough to get into trouble with security."

"When do I get to take them off?"

"When we're in Flint's office."

Through the blackened lenses, Rae appeared to have a bright green beacon on her back, which I followed, dutifully staying between the green lines. I floated in a bubble of silence manufactured by the blinders so that I didn't accidentally overhear anything Libra wanted kept quiet. Which was everything.

After some twisting and turning, Rae closed a door behind me, clicked off the blinders and pulled them from my face. I blinked against the glaring whiteness of the room and squinted at the shadow of a man in front of me.

Wallace Flint perched on the edge of a huge silver desk with his bony shoulders hunched beneath a crisp white lab coat. He glared at me with beady black eyes over his hooked nose and bobbed his bald head like a raven sidling up to a torn trash bag to see what kind of goodies he might find inside. He said, "This is the best you can do?"

"Bubbles Marlowe used to be a detective with the HoloCity Police Department." Rae's voice had an edge when she spoke to him. He wouldn't want to shave with it.

"I hear you've got a problem you want to keep hushed up," I said.

Flint sneered. "These skids have no tact. Are you sure she's up to it? I require the utmost discretion."

Something hardened in the pit of my stomach. To a man like Flint, I wasn't even the trash bag. I was the trash.

"She's good, Flint." Rae picked up a file from Flint's desk and flipped through a sheaf of transparencies inside. "I wouldn't have brought her here if she wasn't."

The glossy white walls seemed to emit an eye-burning light of their own. Transparent charts and holo projections danced behind Flint's head, data he either didn't care if I saw or didn't think I could decipher. Without context it was a meaningless visual babble of numbers and letters and colours. Maybe he turned it on just make himself look clever.

"If you want something from me," I said through gritted teeth, "you talk to me."

His thin lips stiffened as the sneer became a grimace. His beady eyes jumped to Rae. "You're sure about this?"

She nodded and set the file down with one of the transparencies sitting on top. Flint glanced at it. He bobbed his head and licked his lips with a tongue like sandpaper. He picked up the transparency and lifted it up to the white background of the wall to see it more clearly. He raised an eyebrow and put the transparency back in the file. Then he folded his hands before him and cleared his throat.

He said, "I need you to kill a girl."

Chapter Two

I BLINKED AT HIM. Then I turned to Rae and I blinked at her. Neither of them said anything. "You've got to be kidding me," I said.

"This isn't what we talked about, Wally." Rae moved herself slightly between me and the bird man, as if worried one of us might fly at the other.

"It's the only way," Flint said. "I've been thinking about it. It's the only way to be sure she doesn't get it."

"Get what?" I ran a hand through my wet hair and pushed my bangs out of my face so I could glare at him properly. "What is this about?"

"My daughter," Flint said.

"You want me to kill your daughter?"

"Well, my adopted daughter," Flint said. "But no, not her. Her girlfriend."

I laughed but there was no joy in it. "What did the twist do to you?"

"Nothing yet." Flint curled his lip. "That's how I want to keep it."

"Flint's daughter, Angelica Bell, has gotten herself into trouble with a gambling man." Rae passed me a sheet from the file with some outrageous numbers on it. "Owes a fat stack of holocred and won't pay up."

"Can't pay up," Flint snapped. "She doesn't have any money until she turns twenty-one,   and I'm not shelling out."

"Now there's a father figure," I said. "What's it got to do with the twist?"

Rae looked sideways at me. "Angelica's girlfriend is a shill for Mick Vector."

I turned around and put my hand on the door. Vector was the kind of trouble I didn't need. Dodging cops was bad enough without also having to dodge gambling king pins and their ladies of easy virtue. Then I remembered that if I went out there without the blinders, I'd probably be shot dead where I stood. Besides that, I needed the money, and Rae promised Flint was good for a 5K spot. I crossed my arms and faced Flint.

"I'm not killing anyone."

"Angelica turns twenty-one in three weeks," Flint said. "At which point the inheritance from her mother will be hers, and if that red-headed vetch still has her hooks in my daughter—"

"Adopted daughter," I reminded him.

"What difference does it make?" He slammed the palm of his hand on the smooth, shiny surface of the desk.

"You tell me," I said. "You're the one who brought it up."

He narrowed his eyes. "Angelica wants to marry this girl. I won't have it."

"And you think this twist of Angelica's is only interested in settling this debt?"

"She's a shill," Flint said. "Running cons for Vector is her job."

"Mick Vector is a pretty big wig in underground gambling circuits." I tossed the paper with Angelica's numbers back on Flint's desk. It fluttered over the surface and landed on the floor. Flint glowered at me. I said, "He's not the kind of man you skimp on if you like to keep your fingers. But I don't know him for a con man."

A fat vein throbbed over Flint's eyebrow. His lips moved and I had to strain to hear the words. He said, "Are you suggesting this is a coincidence?"

"I'm not suggesting anything. I'll play along. So Vector's placed his shill in Angelica's sights, Angelica falls in love, and when she marries this girl, Vector is going to get what he's owed and then some. Wouldn't it be easier just to pay him off?"

"It's a hundred thousand creds!"

I cracked my knuckles against the metal palm of my upgrade. Flint's black-pebble eyes jumped to the prosthetic, and he stiffened. I took a step forward. "It's a girl's life."

He flinched but held his ground. "I want her out of Angelica's life for good."

"How much is she set to inherit?"

The bird man hunched a little deeper and swallowed. He looked from Rae to me and back to Rae again, his Adam's apple bobbing in his skinny neck. He narrowed his eyes at her. She nodded. He said, "Eight million."

I tried not to faint. "Okay. So peanuts."

"Angelica thinks she's in love." Flint pushed himself off the desk and lurched his way around the other side with the grace of a lame pigeon. "She won't listen to reason."

"This is what you call reason?"

He snapped his eyes to Rae and shouted, "You told me she would help."

"She's a detective." Rae clenched her jaw. "Not a murderer."

"A retired detective," I reminded them both, waving with the prosthetic arm that disqualified me from service with the HCPD. "And I can help you. But I'm not killing anyone."

"I need assurances."

"You need discretion," I said. "You're up for a big promotion, right? The last thing you want is a pretty young thing turning up dead with a finger pointed at you. If anything happens to this girl, you'll be the first one the news feeders jump on. The Trade Zone babies hate that kind of attention. I'll take care of it my own way or not at all."

Flint scowled and threw himself into a high-backed, imitation-leather chair that probably cost more than the real thing. "What's it going to cost me?"

"Five thousand cred," I said. "Plus expenses."

His throat worked over his Adam's apple again, and he drummed his fingers on the desk like he might want to take a hit out on me too. "Fine."

"Tell me about the girl."

Flint spun his chair around and stared at the filing cabinet behind the desk.

Rae rolled her eyes. She said, "Scarlett Martinez. She's a real class piece. One of Vector's best. Beautiful and as far as I can tell, unbesmirchable. Sugar wouldn't melt in her mouth. Parents are dead, but she has a little brother in a private trade school in the Biz District. A real cush placement."

"Could be an angle," I said. "How'd you dig that up?"

"We got a tip." Rae reached into the pocket of her lab coat and passed me a card with a name and address on it.

"Bobby Mook," I said. "I know him. One of Vector's bookies."

"Nervous little guy," Rae said. "But he'll talk on Flint's say so. Thinks he's got a line on Vector we can use to toss the girl."

"If I smear her with the boss, Vector needs a new plan," I said. "It might buy us some time, but Vector's not going to forget a debt that easy. You sure you don't just want to pay him off?"

Flint's chair spun around so fast I was afraid he'd give himself whiplash. "I don't have a hundred thousand cred."

"Angelica has eight million coming her way in three weeks," I said. "And you're a pauper? Doesn't rate with me. If I liked to bet, I'd say it won't rate with Vector either."

"My wife, Angelica's mother, died last year. She made sure Angelica would have everything she needed."

"Except common sense, apparently."

Flint smiled the way a buzzard might smile before it ripped into the intestines of a sun-bloated corpse. "That was never her mother's to give."

"So, what? I'll smear up Scarlett with Angelica and Vector and buy enough time so that she can pay her own debt?"

"That," Flint sighed. "Or I'll pay it with my signing bonus when I get picked up by TZR&D. Once the money is hers, it's on her to protect it. But until then, she's my responsibility."

"Your wife didn't leave you an allowance?"

Flint scowled.

"TZR&D is very competitive," Rae explained.

"I put everything I have into this scouting opportunity," Flint said. "If I don't get the job, I'm busted. Just clean up Angelica's mess. I can't stand the thought of a slime like Vector getting his hands on that money."

"Not when you won't see a single cred of it."

Flint bared his teeth, his thin nostrils flaring. "Can you do it or not?"

His shoulders heaved beneath the white lab coat as he struggled to contain his disdain for me and his eagerness to have the job done. The beady black eyes bore into me like he could see inside me if he stared hard enough. I let him wait. His fingers drummed against the desk like gunfire.

"I want a K spot up front," I said, and his posture deflated with relief. "And get word to Mook that I'm coming."

"You'd better be good for it," Flint said. "I'm paying for results, and I expect to see them promptly."

"If I don't deliver," I said. "You can send flowers to my mother."

Flint sneered again. He was pretty good at it.

"I'll show you out," Rae said.

I inclined my head to her, and she clipped on the headgear. "It's been a pleasure."

"Let's get you outside safely before you get too mushy," Rae said.

Rae became a green dot in a sea of blackness, and I heard the door click open. She left it that way as I followed the green lines toward the exit. I felt Flint's eyes burning into me as I walked away, itching like a rash between my shoulder blades.

"I can see why you like the guy," I said when Rae took my blinders off and led me into the damp alleyway.

"I'll make sure he transfers you the creds," she said. "And thanks. The sooner TZR&D picks that scab off my back, the better."

"I'm relieved it's not a Libra job," I said. "Gamblers and shills I can handle. You scientist types give me the creeps."

"You made that very clear earlier."

"I didn't mean to give you a hard time. I'm just nervous."

"I get it," she said. "We're still good, right? We're miles off Swain's turf."

"Sure," I said. "As long as the girl doesn't end up dead."

Chapter Three

B OBBY MOOK RAN A semi-legit bookkeeping agency on the cusp of the Biz District and the outskirts of the Grit. Flint hadn't paid out my retainer fee yet, so I decided to hoof it rather than shell out for one of the hack pods zipping past me on the maglev grid. Early morning light washed the city in a sickly, off-white haze, but the rain had given up some. HoloPop ads lurched out at me as I passed storefronts, offering me all the things I needed to make my life complete—today it was smart toasters and sexual performance enhancers. Uncanny. I kept my head down and walked through them, keeping my eyes on the narrow strip of pavement next to the grid.

The Biz District didn't have much in the way of sidewalk. Its clientele was strictly made up of the private-boiler-car type. But the strip was whole and unblemished. The black, porous surface collected rainwater to be treated for drinking, solar energy—when the sun deigned to show its face—and the kinetic energy of pedestrian traffic, feeding it all back into the grid. It made for nice walking compared to the cracked and heaving concrete slabs in the Grit District, which was left over from another century and not considered to be worth the cost of maintenance.

I left the glittering black spires of Libra's R&D sector behind me and cut through the financial sector where the massive towers of Trade Zone bean counters, stockbrokers, and day traders acted as a dour wall against the sprawl of the Grit. Elsewhere, the border between the impoverished inner city had been softened by the flow of drugs, illegal tech, and sex workers, allowing the Grit to ooze out of the centre toward other districts like a wave of toxic sludge. The wall of trade buildings, though, was an immutable barricade designed to keep sludge out.

Which meant I made people nervous. Catching a glimpse of myself in the glassy surface of an anonymous holocred pumping institute, I could see why. The sodden imitation fur of my pink jacket made me look as auspicious as a castoff teddy bear stuck in a drainpipe. But the Biz District dealt in cush, not pity. Unless you had creds, you might as well be invisible. The kind of invisible that makes people step anxiously back inside office buildings as you pass. Just as well. Made it a little easier to stay on the sidewalk.

By the time I worked my way out of the towers and into the low-slung stacks of commercial apartments next to the Grit, I was about ready to be seen again. I rang up Mook's number on my tattler and a 'gram of a mousey little man with a pointed nose and jug ears popped up above the wrist of my upgrade.

"This Bobby Mook?" I said.

His eyes flitted from side to side nervously. "Yeah."

"This is Bubbles Marlowe. I'm doing some legwork for a guy called Wallace Flint."

"Yeah?"

"I'm heading in your direction," I said. "Can I come up to talk to you a minute? Flint told you I was coming?"

"Sure." He twitched. "Sure. Yeah."

He didn't wait for further pleasantries. My tattler blinked and Mook's face was replaced with the spinning icon for PingComm, my half-rate service provider. I shrugged and dropped the upgrade to my side. Nice chat.

Before hitting Mook's joint, I ducked into a convenience strip for something to eat. It was more like an alley with vending machines wedged in between dumpsters, but transparent awnings provided some shelter from the spatter of rain. I plugged a couple credit chips into the NRG soda machine and cracked the tab while I browsed the selection. Noodle bowls and imitation sausages held little appeal this early in the day. I chugged the energy drink, lobbed the can into a recycling chute, and grabbed a Kreme Kween donut covered in bubble-gum-pink frosting and rainbow sprinkles. Breakfast of champions.

Coming out of the alley, I almost ran into a man with a transparent overcoat covering an expensive black suit. He wore a grey hat pulled low over his eyes, but his wide mouth scowled at me. Hard to ignore the riffraff when they plow right into you. He side-stepped, expertly avoiding the puddle collecting where the porous sidewalk ended and the concrete began, and slipped inside a building whose ground floor proclaimed it to be Glitter Haus, a nightclub fashion wholesaler that recycled last decade's styles into trash even the Grit District pro skirts wouldn't wear.

The haphazard stack of portable apartments that made up Mook's office building looked like something a giant toddler had constructed. Siding in various shades of dingy blue and grey clashed with each other in a recycled patchwork of not-quite-flush corners and edges. Dull neon signs blinked and flickered beneath years of smog residue outside every peephole sized window. A sign for Bargain Bookkeeping, half lit and missing most of its letters, flickered on the third floor. Dark patches on the wall filled in the blanks with ghost letters, but the sign seemed to read Bar Bokee from the street.

I licked the last of the icing off my fingers, wiped them on my jacket, and stepped into the narrow vestibule. Inside, thin light filtered through the scuffed plastic windows, illuminating a faded directory of the various services offered within. At the bottom I read: B. Mook, Bookkeeping, Suite 317B. I opened the door into a dirty grey corridor filled with nondescript doors beneath black, stencilled unit numbers. One of the doors opened, and a wizened old man in green scrubs peeked out beneath a sign that read Vitality

Technologies. He worked his jaw back and forth as if testing to see if any words might pop out. When they didn't, he receded back inside his hole in the wall and closed the door.

The stairwell to my right barely had enough room to turn around inside and twisted sharply enough that, by the time I'd made the fifteen or so necessary rotations to make it to the third floor, my Kreme Kween donut threatened to evacuate. I pushed through the doorway into another dirty grey corridor and knocked on the door of unit 317B.

No answer.

I pinged Mook on my tattler again. It rang until an answering service picked up. The sound echoed in the hallway and on the other side of the door like a poorly recorded audio file. I let it go until the beep, then killed the call and tried the handle.

Bargain Bookkeeping was open for business. The thin door swung open to reveal a tiny, dark reception area. A narrow brown desk sat in the centre of the room with a clunky computer monitor angled to one side. Two dented, beige filing cabinets stood behind the desk like weary sentinels with drawers that didn't quite close all the way and the yellowing corner of some ancient document poking out of one of the seams. Above the desk, a bare dome light glowed with a dull yellow light. A tacky, painted metal sign on the desk read Administration. Other than the faint hum of the resting computer, the place was silent. Downstairs, somebody stomped along a corridor and slammed a door.

At the back of the room, tucked in next to the filing cabinets, was a door about the right size for a supply closet. Another painted metal sign proclaimed this to be Office.

I said, "Mook?"

The door didn't open. I went over and listened to the silence on the other side. Knocked. Nothing. I tried the handle and it turned, so I opened the door and stepped inside.

The place had probably been a supply closet before Mook put on some airs and decided he needed his own private mouse hole. A side table with scratched brown paint acted as a desk that took up most of the claustrophobic space. An acidic tang hung in the air, sweat and ammonia and something else. Atop the desk, an open ledger sprawled across the surface, covering the entire thing. Little neat letters and numbers filled the pages. The pen that had scratched them lay on the floor. A stale looking pastry sat on a thin paper plate on the edge of the desk, untouched. The stained, grey fabric of an ancient task chair squeezed into the back corner as if it had been knocked aside. A scuffed grey shoe peeked out the side of the desk. I sidled around the edge and looked underneath.

If it wasn't for the thin strands of colourless hair scraped across his spotty scalp, Mook could have been a child dressed up in Daddy's suit. Brown fabric bagged around his knees and elbows, and the yellowing collar of a once-white shirt pulled tight against his throat where it had caught against the height adjustment lever of the little chair. He'd fallen like a broken doll, cast aside for something brighter and flashier. A dark stain crept out from beneath one threadbare sleeve and a sour taste flooded into my mouth.

I knelt next to the little man and felt his wrist for a pulse. His skin was clammy and not quite cool, but nothing flickered beneath the surface. He held a crumpled piece of paper in his left hand, which I removed. It would have been nice if this had held some clue, but it was just a scrap of paper with my name on it, written in the same neat handwriting that filled the ledger above.

The nerves in my left shoulder twinged beneath the upgrade, and my metal hand balled into a fist. I closed my eyes, took a deep breath in, and exhaled slowly, trying to relax the muscles that sent biofeedback into the prosthetic. Rae had said it would stop happening once the wound had healed and I was more used to wearing the arm, but every time the upgrade seized up on me it was like a punch in the gut. A reminder that Chief Swain had won. He'd shut me up and taken a piece of me that I'd never get back. My throat ached, and I swallowed against a dryness I thought might never leave. Then I stuffed the paper in my pocket and looked around the rest of the space.

Nothing caught my eye. Nothing worth the life of this nervous mouse of a man, no matter how pitiful a life it was. I backed out of the supply closet and wiped down the door handle. The reception area held nothing of interest either. A couple paper receipts for takeout food were balled up in the wire waste bin beneath the desk. A calendar marked today and tomorrow as "Judy Off," which I supposed was why there was no receptionist here to protect Mook from the repercussions of wheeling and dealing with the wrong crowd. I glanced at the computer monitor, but in the centre of the screen was a small box requesting a password. Deciding there was nothing more I could do, I wiped down anything I thought I'd touched and closed the door behind me.

The corridor was still dirty and grey and just as empty as before. I took the back stairs down and out into the alley. As far as I could tell, no one had seen me. I put my head down and hurried through the alley toward the Grit.

Chapter Four

I CHECKED THE FILE Rae had sent me on Scarlett Martinez's luxury apartment in Gibson Heights, a platinum security haven for highbinder politicians, district kings, and celebrity feedcasters. How she afforded to rent a place in the Heights was beyond me, but I suspected she did more for Mick Vector than collect errant loan payments. Getting past security to talk to her was going to be tough enough without looking like a drowned lab rat. I decided I'd better head back to my flat to change.

My building was one of the few left standing in the old warehouse sector on the eastern edge of the Grit. There weren't many people in my neighbourhood at this time of day. Those few who wandered around looked as if they'd been at it since last night, stumbling from stoop to recessed stoop to rest their weary bones in the relative cover of torn awnings and crumbling doorways. The block out front of my squat, grey-faced building with its board-blinded eyes was deserted. I avoided going in the faded red door facing street side. It had been torn off the hinges months ago, and the superintendent had simply propped it back into the door frame rather than fix it. The thing was as liable to crush me as let me pass, so I keyed in my code for the electronic lock at the side entrance, which opened to a staircase of crumbling steps covered in torn carpeting so stained it was hard to imagine it was once blue. At least, I think it was blue.

The keypad into my actual apartment was in worse shape than the front door; it had been broken a couple weeks before my "accident." I had thought it was the usual kind of break and enter in this neighbourhood. A smash and grab. I had nothing of value to grab so it was more like a smash and smash. The place had been trashed, but it wasn't much better before so I hadn't bothered reporting it. I'd put a repair request in to the super, but getting him to act on it was a bit like trying to tie a shoestring on a bottle fly.

Looking back, I figure it was some of Swain's goons—maybe in uniform and maybe not—checking the place out to see if I'd been working after hours on Whip Tesla's drug case. Normally I was too soused to give a second thought to work once I clocked out. That's what Swain had liked about me. But the Tesla case was different. We'd let Tesla go. Less than twenty-four hours later, Tropical Punch hit the streets and my friend Jimi Ng, Rae's boyfriend, OD'd on the pinch ... I obsessed over it. It was my fault. I kept asking questions, had to know the truth. Swain didn't like that quite as much. Must have hit a nerve though. The next time I hit the training circuit, my brand-new plasma rifle overcharged, blew up, and took half of me with it. I wasn't dead, but I'd never work for the HCPD again.

I tried the keypad, just for fun. It made a pained squealing noise that grated on my eardrums like electronic feedback. I punched the thing with my metal fist and the shattered remains of the number pad tinkled to the floor of the hallway. Thanks, Swain. I needed a new one anyway. I pushed the door into my apartment open and stepped inside.

A little black-and-white cat peered around the wall into the living room and blinked at me disdainfully with half-lidded, yellow eyes. It said, "You woke me up. I was in the middle of an upgrade."

"So sorry, your highness." I slammed the door closed behind me and threw my sodden jacket over the back of a saggy armchair I'd rescued from the dumpster behind Anachronism Antiques. The jacket was an improvement. The rest of the apartment looked like something coughed up by a disgruntled waste-disposal bot with a personality disorder. A nice place if you liked asymmetry and grease stains. The cat padded over and sniffed at my feet.

"Where have you been?" It reached forward on long black legs with little white mittens on each end, arching its back and pushing its tail into the air. "I was worried."

I scratched the base of its tail and felt the tingle of nanoparticle feedback of the SmartPet's cat-skin. It purred.

"The hell you were," I said.

"You're supposed to check in every eight hours when you aren't in the apartment," the cat said and sniffed at the sleeve of my jacket, which hung over the edge of the chair and onto the floor. It glared balefully at me. "It's been ten and a half. I'll have to report this."

"I know, I know." I crouched down and let it take a handful of biometric readings for my file. "I'm clean. I was just delayed."

Mittens the Kitten was a certified, addictions-recovery model SmartPet I'd shelled out for after drying out in the hospital and decided I should probably try to keep it that way. I might be lying low as far as Swain and the HCPD were concerned, but I hadn't forgotten what I owed the Chief of Police. Getting sober after years of casual abuse wasn't something I thought I could do on my own. Coming home after work to an empty apartment had been bad enough. Being trapped in an empty apartment, alone and jobless, while I recovered from the explosion and subsequent surgery was more than I could take. Rae had suggested the SmartPet. I'd thought it was silly, but I knew I had to do something. I wanted revenge, and drunks don't make very good vigilantes. In any case, I had been surprised how much I enjoyed the little jerk's company.

Mittens put its paws on my knees and stretched its little pink nose up to touch mine. The nanoparticles were cold and tingly. The cat blinked slowly, registering and recording the record for my personal file. Satisfied, it stalked back toward the charging base in my bedroom. "I need to finish my update. Need anything?"

"Do I have any clothes that don't make me look like a washed up pro skirt?"

The cat made a noise like it was hacking up a hairball. I realized it was laughing. "I didn't want to say anything, but . . ."

"Hey, my lifestyle got an upgrade. I'm still working on the wardrobe." I stalked into the bedroom, tore my damp clothes off, and left them in a pile on the floor. "But Rae found me a job."

"As a hooker?" The cat batted a paw at the pile of laundry.

"Investigative work," I said, and threw a wet sock at the SmartPet. "I need to get into Gibson Heights and—"

"And those guys use class dolls."

"I'm not hooking."

"Look." Mittens yawned up at me. "You're not getting into a high-cush compound like the Heights with your wardrobe as anything but a pro skirt. You might not even be able to pull that off."

I rummaged through my closet for anything that wasn't covered in sequins, transparent panels, or imitation fur. I cursed. "Did I really think I looked good in this crap?"

"I'm not sure what kind of exam you have to pass in order to buy your own clothing," Mitten said. "But I think you skipped the certification process."

"I need normal clothes," I said. "Plain clothes."

"You need cush."

I brought up my credit accounts on my tattler and checked to see if Flint had deposited the retainer yet. Nothing. I cursed again and pinged Rae. No answer. "Well I don't have any."

I found a sleeveless black dress at the back of my closet with a hideous tulle skirt and a neckline that looked like it might be diving for my belly button. I tore off the bottom half and grabbed a pair of standard issue HCPD uniform trousers in dark grey that I'd forgotten to hand in when I got retired.

"It's not awful," the cat said after I finished buttoning the pants. "But you'll never get past security on your own. You should call Dickie."

Dickie. Why hadn't I thought of that? "You're a genius."

"Compared to you," the cat said, and flopped onto its side to bat at the iridescent tulle skirt I'd dropped on the floor. "But that's setting the bar pretty low."

I ignored the cat and pinged Dickie Roh. Dickie comes from money. His parental units run a wildly successful PornoPop franchise out of the HoloCity Biz District. Big money. I met Dickie back in my days on the Grit beat. I'd busted up a hive of wanna-be gangsters who'd tried to level up their criminal game and failed. Kidnapping can be a quick and easy way to make money in HoloCity, but you've got to be big-time enough to be heard. Poor Dickie had been hanging upside down in a makeshift cell for a week when I'd found him, and his parents hadn't even noticed he was missing. The thieves were too small-time to know what to do about it. Dickie never did go home after that. He hung around the station for a while, trying to get my number. Eventually I gave in. Other than Rae, Dickie is the only friend of mine to stick around through the mess of my accident and the even bigger mess of getting sober. He had some strange ideas about going into business together that I'd avoided so far, but maybe it was time.

He picked up instantly, his eager round face popping out of my tattler like an old-fashioned jack-in-the-box. "Bubbles Marlowe! To what do I owe the pleasure?"

"Cut the crap, Dick. I need your help."

His black eyes disappeared into little crescents above his round cheeks as he grinned from ear to ear. He rubbed his hands together in front of his face. "You talked to Rae."

I groaned. "I should have known you had something to do with this."

"I'm telling you, P.I. work is perfect for retired cops," he said. "You know the streets. You know the brass—"

"The brass is trying to kill me, Dick," I said. "And everyone on the streets remembers me as either a cop or a drunk. They don't exactly trust me."

"You have that cool arm now, though. You're a cyborg, Bubs. With boobs. People will pay top cred for a cyborg detective."

"With boobs."

He nodded enthusiastically. "Let me do your marketing. I've got spreadsheets—"

"I need to get into Gibson Heights."

Dickie's smile faded. "The Heights? The job rates then, huh? That's tricky."

"Do your parents still live there?"

"Sure." He rubbed the back of his neck with a pudgy hand. "But I haven't really talked to them since . . ."

"Does security know? Could you get me inside?"

"I don't know. Maybe. At least they won't shoot me for trying. Probably."

"Please?"

Dickie squeezed his eyes shut and scrunched up his face like he'd eaten the daily special at Rikki Tikki Takeout. He opened one eye and said, "I want to be on the case."

"It's not a case, Dickie. I'm just doing a favour for Rae."

"You don't have to let me interrogate anyone." Dickie gesticulated wildly and the background of his 'gram lurched and swayed. "But I can help. Behind the scenes, like. And I have a hat you could wear."

"You'll help me?"

"I'm already in the boiler."

"You have your own car?"

"I'll call when I'm outside," he said, and hung up on me.

I sighed and ran a hand through my hair. Mittens pawed at my pant leg and I looked down.

"Did you fill out my warranty documentation?" The cat licked one of its paws and then yawned, exposing two long canines. "The section specific to disposal of the companion in the case of—"

"You're worried I'm going to kack it?"

"Not exactly," the cat said, then padded over to the circular charging disk in the corner of my bedroom. "As long you aren't drunk, I've fulfilled my contract."

"Whoever wrote your code was a prick, you know that?"

Mittens shrugged. "I'm a cat."

"I should have gone with Buster the excruciatingly positive bunny."

Mittens blinked at me one last time. "Upgrade time. Try not to die."

The skin blinked off. I threw a pillow at the spherical bot. It wasn't as satisfying as I'd thought it would be.

Chapter Five

DICKIE AND I sat outside Gibson Heights in his personal boiler car. The car, a slick black maglev pod, looked like it belonged in the neighbourhood. In the hat and jacket he'd brought me, I almost looked like I did too. The jacket did a pretty good job of hiding the upgrade, which was a bonus. High-cush joints like the Heights usually required preregistration of cybernetic enhancements and special licensing for anything that might be used to mishandle, maim, or murder one of their high-paying guests. Dickie assured me that he had an in through security, and that he'd made a deal so they wouldn't scan me.

"Are you sure this is a good idea?" I looked up at the glittering dome of translucent solar screens. I only saw one entrance.

"It'll be fine." Dickie leaned back in the buttery leather seats. "Me and Hawkins go way back. But don't mess it up. He wants my car as collateral."

I pulled on a black glove to cover my metal hand and put Dickie's hat on my head. "How do I look?"

"Like you just stepped out of an Old Earth noir film." Dickie grinned. "You ooze private eye."

"Do I need antibiotics for that?" I glanced at my reflection in the window of the boiler. "I feel like a hitman."

"Might not be a bad impression to give," Dickie said. Then he told the car to call security.

The entrance to the dome split open into a series of triangular panels and spun open like the iris of a mechanical eye. The boiler slid silently into the opening of a pitch-black interior chamber and lurched to the left. Dickie winced. "I guess we're taking the scenic route."

"Why are we moving sideways?"

"Hawkins must have keyed us into the lower-level garage," Dickie said. "Makes sense. Less traffic down there. He's not supposed to let me back on the premises."

"Why is he risking his job to help us?"

"He's risking his job for a chance to score my car." Dickie's usually jovial face tightened in a joyless smile. "You may have some trouble from security once you're on your own."

"Great," I said. "Thanks for the heads up. Who is this guy?"

"We used to gamble. When I lived here. He lost some money, and I left before he had a chance to win it back. I think he thinks I ghosted him on purpose."

"Well, I hope he won't be too broken-hearted if he gets beat again."

Dickie shrugged. "You bring a gun?"

"I haven't used a gun since—"

"Okay." Dickie peered out the window into the blackness as the car dropped down to another level. "Okay. If it comes to it, he takes the car."

"Still want to be a detective?"

A sheen of sweat had broken out on Dickie's forehead, faintly illuminated by the glow of the interior lights. "I always liked the down-and-out ones best."

The lights in the garage came on in a jarring burst of white, dimmed slightly by the tinted glass windows of the boiler car, but bright enough to make me jump. A guy in a black suit banged on the top of the car with the palm of his hand, and Dickie pushed a button. The doors opened like the wings of a shiny black beetle, and Dickie and I stepped out into the garage.

"Long time no see, Mr. Roh." Hawkins looked me up and down through a pair of black visilens glasses. Thin tubes ran from the arms of the glasses, curved behind his ears and then spiralled inside to an invisible cochlear comm implant. He nodded almost imperceptibly. "This is your friend?"

I shifted my weight so that my upgrade was behind me a little in case he was scanning. "I need to see Scarlett Martinez."

Hawkins flipped up his glasses. The spirals remained in his ears, but the lenses split away to rest on the top of close-cropped curls. Brown skin feathered slightly between his eyebrows, and his dark eyes were like empty black wells. Slowly, he smiled. He had very fine, very white teeth.

"Nobody sees Miss Martinez unless she asks for them."

Dickie groaned. "Come on, Hawkins. You said you could get us in."

"You are in." Hawkins' voice had a dangerous edge to it. "But you aren't getting up to see Miss Martinez."

"My boss isn't going to like that," I said.

Hawkins curled a lip around his pretty teeth and leaned toward me conspiratorially. He whispered, "And who might that be?"

"Mick Vector sent me," I said. Hawkins snapped back like I'd slapped him. "It's a time sensitive matter."

Dickie pulled at his collar and bugged out his eyes at me. "Vector? You didn't tell me you were—"

"Is that so?" Hawkins smiled wider. His eyes darted over me again. "Do you have any proof?"

"Why don't you call him yourself," I said. "You can tell him you're the one holding up the message."

Hawkins looked a bit nervous then. "If you're lying, I'll lose my job."

"Dickie," I said. "Sweeten the deal."

"I'm already leaving the car as collateral!"

"You take me up alone," I said. "Dick and the car stay here. And while you wait, you can play another game of ... What was it, Dickie? The last game you won?"

"Matgo, but—"

"That's two chances on the car," I said. "Just to let me deliver a message."

The parking garage was full of neatly stacked boiler cars, mostly steel and gunmetal blue. Dickie's little black number was nicer than a lot of them. Could be the rest were guest cars—I didn't know a lot about personal boilers; I could barely afford to rent a hack pod—but I had a feeling Dickie's ride was worth some cush, even in the Heights.

Hawkins licked his lips. "Why didn't Vector send one of his regular guys?"

"Why don't you call up and see if she'll see me. She'll see me."

He stood there, frozen with indecision.

I said, "Get in the car, Dick. I'll come back with Vector."

"Wait a minute now." Hawkins growled to cover his nerves. "I'll call."

He gave a voice command and flipped the visilenses down so Dickie and I couldn't see the doll when she picked up. Hawkins turned away from me anyway. A stupid move if I'd been carrying, but maybe he'd scanned and knew I wasn't. The upgrade wasn't armed, even if it could be considered a weapon alone. I could have broken his neck.

His growl softened into something he probably used to talk to kittens and little old ladies, "Miss Martinez? It's Hawkins. Sorry to bother you. Yes. Heights Security. Sure, we've met. Yes. Yes, I'm sure you do. It's all right. Say, there's a broad here to see you. Says she's got a message from Mick Vector. I didn't want to let her up, but she's insisting I call. Yeah, Vector. No, I don't know her.

All right. Sure. Yeah. Thank you, Miss Martinez. Sorry to bother you."

I clenched my upgrade into a fist against my thigh. Dickie watched me with his eyes wide. He shook his head slightly. Sweat stains blossomed under his arms, turning the slick grey fabric of his dress shirt black.

"She'll see you," Hawkins said, and I almost hit him anyway.

I was so sure my plan wasn't going to work.

I relaxed my arm and said, "Of course she will."

"I'll have one of the boys escort you," Hawkins said. He made a brief call, then he turned to Dickie and reached into the inner pocket of his black jacket. Dickie flinched when he saw what was in Hawkins' thin brown fingers. "This time, Mr. Roh, we use my deck."

Another black-suited security goon appeared from behind the guard shack at the centre of the garage. He was at least twice as big as Hawkins and not half as pretty to look at. His wide, pink neck oozed out of the tight collar like putty, and his face had the flat, dull look of someone who made his living getting punched.

Hawkins said, "Mungo here'll show you up."

Dickie narrowed his eyes at me. "Rest up, Bubbles. It's going to be a long walk back to the Grit."

I tried to smile reassuringly at Dickie, but it came out more like a grimace. Then I followed Mungo toward the lift with a pit in my stomach. Could be he was leading me to a quiet place where he planned to clock me and leave me for roach food, but Gibson Heights probably didn't tolerate roaches. Just in case, I stayed on his right and kept the upgrade between us. I had never used it in a fight. It barely did what I wanted it to when I was standing still, but I figured I had a better chance of lumping him up accidentally this way, if I flailed and fell over when he attacked me.

Mungo led me inside a tiny white box. The two of us fit inside like a pair of tinned sausages. Mungo took up more than his fair share of the air and filled the rest of it with a smell like onion peels and spoiled milk. I sucked shallow breaths through my teeth and told myself not to cry. He keyed in a complex series of numbers on the manual keypad inside the box.

"Impressive." I decided to try to alleviate the tension the old-fashioned way. By making an ass of myself. "How long did it take to memorize that?"

Mungo grunted noncommittally.

"You know the Martinez dame?"

Another grunt.

"Silent type, huh?" I flicked up the collar on my coat as if that might protect me from the swamp gas oozing out of his pores. "Me too. Never know when you're going to say something that gets you in trouble."

Mungo slammed his hand against the keypad, wrenched the sliding door open with a paw the size of my head, and grunted again.

"I'll try it now," I said. "Lips zipped. Case in point."

Mungo put his meat paw on the back of my neck and pushed me into a long corridor made of transparent concrete blocks illuminated by internal lights in variegated colours. Ghost-like shadows moved on the other side of the blocks, becoming flesh toned the closer they came to the wall. I was starting to get an idea of the kind of work Scarlett Martinez did for Mick Vector. I looked away from a cluster of intertwined bodies which, through the glaze of the concrete, looked like an abstract sculpture made of disembodied limbs. Impossible to tell which bits belonged to which or where they were going.

Mungo kept his eyes forward and walked me down to the end of the hall, where he stopped at a narrow black door with the number nineteen on it in small golden digits. He rapped on the door twice and stood where the security camera could clearly see his face. He rattled off another long alpha numerical code I didn't have a hope of remembering, stepped aside, and pushed me forward. A buzzer sounded inside the apartment and the door opened.

A tall, bronze-skinned woman in a trim, white pantsuit opened the door. The blouse beneath the fine lines of her jacket was little more than fine mesh, displaying the ample curves of her statuesque body. Long, red hair fell in sculpted waves over the shoulder of her suit like a tide of blood washing over a bone white shore. Full lips, painted a burgundy so deep it was almost black, spread in a wide smile over neat white teeth. She said, "Vector, huh?"

I glanced at the lump of meat beside me and shrugged.

"Drift," she said to Mungo. "I can handle it from here."

Mungo obeyed without a grunt and moved silently through the hall of flittering ghosts, back toward the elevator. For a big guy, he was pretty light on his feet.

"So." Scarlett Martinez breathed out with a contented sigh, and her lip curled up on one side. "Why are you really here?"

"I'd like to speak to you." I swallowed, feeling intensely conscious of how fatale her femme act might just be. "On behalf of—"

"Come inside before you start talking business," she said, and opened the door the rest of the way. I stepped inside the apartment and the door swung closed behind me with a hydraulic hush. The air inside was warm and sweet with a milky haze settling in uneven layers as if somewhere, someone was chain-smoking kretek. The walls of the apartment were covered in a textured, burgundy velvet and were reflected in infinite repetition within two strategically placed mirrors. Tiny things, each about the size of my own flat.

Miss Martinez swayed her way over to a long, smoked-glass side table with the flared legs of her otherwise painted on trousers gently swishing behind her like the tail of an exotic bird. She removed the top from a crystal decanter and poured a deep-red liquid into a glass like cascading fractals. "Drink?"

"I can't—" I swallowed the thickness in my throat and tried again. "I don't drink," I said. "Not anymore."

"You must be terribly dehydrated." She peered coquettishly over her shoulder at me from beneath heavily made-up eyelashes.

My cheeks burned, and I felt a cold prickle along the back of my neck. My heart beat faster. I couldn't decide if I was embarrassed or excited. Martinez wasn't my type, but my desire to be like her licked sensuously down my spine and settled somewhere between my thighs. I said, "I could stand some water."

She bent forward, displaying her muscular buttocks and hamstrings, and reached inside a hidden compartment beneath the table. When she turned back to me, she held her own glass in one hand and a slender blue bottle of chilled lunar water that probably cost more than my HCPD salary. She gestured to a low chaise lounge wrapped in a fabric like woven cream and placed our drinks on a little glass tray next to it. She perched her shapely rear upon the raised section of the lounge and patted the lower section beside her.

I sat. The weight of my prosthetic hung heavily from my left shoulder. Next to Martinez, I felt clunky. Not just less feminine, but less human than the divine specimen next to me. I reached for the bottle, unscrewed the cap, and took a long drink of liquid cush. It lacked the tang of the filtered rainwater from HoloCity's water-treatment facility, which was expensive enough. Compared to the unfiltered poison most residences in the Grit were used to, it wasn't even in the same chemical family. The more expensive it was, the less it tasted of anything but money.

Scarlett Martinez turned toward me with her glass cradled in her hand and said, "On behalf of whom?"

"Excuse me?"

"You came here on behalf of someone, you said. And we both know it wasn't Vector."

"Right," I said and took a deep breath. "I've been sent here by Wallace Flint."

A chill entered the room at Flint's name, and Martinez stiffened. "Flint," she said.

"I have a deal to propose."

"A deal from Flint?" Her dark eyes slid over my face and across the long black jacket Dickie had lent me. It didn't linger anywhere. There wasn't much to look at. "Why should I listen to anything that man has to say?"

"How much would it cost for you to remove your hooks from young Angelica Bell?"

"Hooks?" She sneered at me. It was a lot less pretty than her smile. The eyes above were like shards of obsidian, ready to slice. "What makes you say hooks?"

"Come on, Scarlett." I placed the bottle of water back on the tray and leaned toward her a little. "You don't care for the girl, do you? Vector's looking to settle a score and you're the shill."

She turned away from me. "Flint would think something like that."

"What'll it cost? He's a tight one, but I think we can settle this without anyone's reputation getting hurt."

"Reputation?" She whirled and pierced me with those polished stone irises. "Flint doesn't give a gutter-rat's ass for anyone's reputation but his own. He's not looking to pay me off."

"He's no cookie." I rolled my metal shoulder and felt the fingers spasm. "But that doesn't make Angelica fair play."

"Angelica is a hard pinch," Martinez said. "She drinks and gambles too much. She owes Mick more than a hundred K stacks. But I don't blame her for it."

"Well, Vector seems to," I said. "And he's keen to have his accounts settled. Is that why he hired Mook?"

She laughed softly. "Hired whom?"

"Bobby Mook," I said. "A mousey little runt on the outskirts of the Grit, did some bookkeeping. Maybe a little blackmailing. He got his card punched this morning. Didn't even have time to finish his breakfast."

She wore a look of studied indifference. She let her eyes slide back up to my face and licked her lips again. I didn't know how she kept the lipstick on. "What does it have to do with me?"

"I thought maybe you could tell me."

"You think Mick would do a thing like that?" She laughed again. "I suppose that's what you told the uniforms when they turned up."

"They didn't," I said. "I didn't call it in."

She appraised me coolly and said, "That's an interesting little tidbit, isn't it?"

"I'm getting a K stack as a retainer," I said. "It's yours if you lay off the Bell girl."

"Are you really?" She seemed amused by the thought. "Have you learned to bleed the stone?"

"I don't want this to get ugly."

"It's already ugly," she said. "What did you say your name was?"

"Marlowe," I said. "Bubbles Marlowe."

"Of course. Now, did Flint tell you what he did to my mother, Marlowe? Ten years of research stolen, and her position with Libra. And that's just the intellectual theft. The rest ..." She took a long drink from her glass and licked her lips delicately. "She couldn't live with what he left of her. And yes, when I met Angelica, I had all those things in my mind. I have a brother, you know. I'd love to put him through school on Flint's dime. I thought of it."

"Let's come together on a price," I said. "And leave the girl out of it."

"Or what?" She sipped her drink and turned to me with her lips glistening and her dark eyes ablaze. The sickly sweetness of the liquid wafted toward me in the thick air and awoke a different kind of thirst. "You'll tell the cops what you think you know about Mick's bookie? What makes you think the girl wants to be out of it? Maybe we're in love."

I snorted. "Come on, Scarlett. I know what you're doing."

"Do you? Wallace Flint destroyed my family, and if I have to tear up his to get what's mine, so be it. I happen to be very fond of Angelica, as a matter of fact. And she's not so hot on her daddy, so—"

"Stepfather," I said. "He was very clear about that."

The scent of her drink was making my skin crawl. I reached into a pocket and the woman's eyes went wide. She flinched, but I held out a hand with a stick of gum in it. I unwrapped it, tucked the wrapper back into my pocket and put the stick in my mouth, chewing thoughtfully. "Flint's not all that torn up about it from what I saw."

"You don't think—" She stopped herself and smiled again, slow and luxurious. She shrugged. "No, I suppose not. He wouldn't tell you."

I didn't feel like playing her game, and I said so. She laughed, making a sound like water running through the gutter. "Well, I'm not doing your job for you, 'Detective.' You can take your offer and choke on it. Angelica is mine, and I hope it destroys the old bastard."

"Would you say that if she was here?"

The smile crept even wider across the burgundy painted lips and there was something else in her eyes now. A clicking noise behind me made my heart stop. I turned slowly to stare into the single dead-eye of a small black pistol. Angelica Bell said, "He is an old bastard. And I'll marry whomever I please."

Angelica was no angel. As tall as me and twice as broad with hard muscle showing through her thin grey shirt. Subdermal implants made spiralling patterns over her skin that rippled with shadow in the low light. Her black hair was cut as if with rusty scissors and tossed carelessly to one side, revealing a shaved skull underneath with more implants there. She had a handsome face with strong features, hardened by the steel in her eyes, and twisted by something I couldn't read and didn't want to.

"Time to drift," she whispered. "You can tell Flint I don't need any help from him anymore. I'm a big girl now."

"Yes, you are," I said to the pistol. I put my hands up and stood slowly. I took a step sideways, away from the chaise lounge, to give myself a bit of room. "Put the gun down, Angelica, please."

"It's please, now, is it?" She sneered. "Did my daddy say please?"

I lunged for the gun and crushed her hand against it with my metal fist. Angelica shouted.

"Ruin her, baby," Scarlett said from behind me.

I felt a cool breeze as the air in the room shifted and then a noise like shattering glass. It took me a moment to realize the sound had come from the explosion of pain at the back of my head. Angelica laughed and brought her left fist up into the side of my jaw. Then she howled as my upgrade spasmed and her fingers snapped in my hand. The room spun around me and I put both my hands out to steady myself, letting go of her broken fingers. The gun fell to the floor with no sound at all.

I spun downward, slowly, like a piece of trash caught in the wind, and when I fell onto the plush carpet, I was staring at the gun again. I groaned and rolled over and the mirrored glass lights of the ceiling danced for me. Then Angelica's fist drove the message home and didn't leave any room for miscommunication. Unconsciousness opened its fetid, black mouth and I let it swallow me.

Chapter Six

W HEN I CAME TO, the lights had been switched off and the apartment was silent. I peeled myself up off the ground and put a hand to my jaw where the angel had clobbered me. It wasn't too bad. I probably wouldn't need surgery, and I always did like my right side a little lumpy.

I stumbled over to the wall and turned the lights on. I was alone. My ears felt like they were full of water. I worried that maybe Angelica had busted something inside my brain. But I shook my head and didn't feel any loose screws bouncing around. I realized it was just the room—with its plush carpet, velvet walls, and smoky air—that made me feel like I was being held under water.

The sitting room was empty but for the melted spheroid furniture in the same off-white colour as the chaise lounge I had taken a nap under. Warm light glittered off the smoked-glass fixtures in the ceiling, the tables strewn around the room. No outside light came in. I peeked into the tiny kitchenette. Refrigerator empty except for a couple of takeout containers. A pair of wooden chopsticks rested in the sink. Counters clean enough to eat off of, which was a pretty good indication that never happened. No table. I pictured Angelica and her high-cush fiancée eating noodles over the sink. It didn't rate.

On the opposite side of the apartment was the bedroom. Angelica must have been hiding in there, waiting for the right moment to ruin me, as the Martinez dame had so eloquently put it. I poked around the drawers, under the bed, in the tiny but elegant bathroom. Nothing of interest. Eventually I decided to take my aching head back down to the parking garage to see if Dickie had made out any better than I had. I turned the lights off again, opened the door into the corridor, and let it lock behind me.

A bigger lump than the one on my jaw stood outside the door.

"I hope I didn't keep you waiting," I said.

Mungo grunted and led me toward the elevator again. I shrugged and followed. Some service in this place. We reversed course through the compound. Inside the little, white box again. I hardly noticed the smell this time, distracted as I was by the pain in my head.

"What's the smoke, Bubbles?" Dickie's panicked voice greeted me as the lift door opened, and I stumbled into the garage. "What took you so long?"

"You sound like my SmartPet," I muttered. "Do we still have a ride or are we doing the walk of shame?"

Hawkins stepped out from behind Dickie with a tight smile on his face. "It's good to see you again, Marlowe. I take it your visit was a success?"

He didn't look all that happy to see me.

"I delivered my message, if that's what you mean," I said. "And then Angelica Bell delivered me from my wits. You failed to mention that Miss Martinez had a visitor."

He sneered. "You failed to ask."

"My mistake." I rubbed my jaw. "It's been swell, gentlemen. Literally."

Dickie looked a little pale around his nose and mouth, and beads of sweat poured down the side of his face. "I think we should go now, Bubbles."

Mungo cracked his knuckles casually and leaned against the front of the boiler car like he meant to stay there.

"Sure," I said. "Which way to the exit?"

Hawkins glared at me with his visilenses propped up on his head. He opened the doors on the boiler- with a sour look on his face and pushed Dickie inside by the scruff of his neck. He turned to me and said, "You're not walking this time, but if that little cheat shows up here again, he's getting parted out. Don't come back."

"Invitation only," I promised.

I slipped into the car after Dickie. The doors slammed and everything went black. The car lurched back onto the maglev track. We sat in the darkness and silence with only Dickie's fear-sweat stink to keep us company.

When the track spit us back out into the street, I was surprised to see the sun was still up behind the thick fog of overcast clouds. Dickie keyed in the coordinates to my flat, leaned back in the seat, and rubbed his face. "On second thought, that was a terrible idea."

"You won, didn't you?" I said. "And I didn't start any fights."

"By the skin of my teeth," he said. "Didn't put me in Hawkins' good books, either. He's probably going to put a hit on me just to save face. And your face is pretty messed up for someone who didn't get in a fight."

"I said I didn't start it," I said. "Angelica finished it before I even knew I was in the ring. At least she had the decency not to call it in, or we would be limping home."

"I changed my mind." Dickie sighed. "I'm not really cut out of the sleuthing business. You can keep the jacket. It looks better on you."

"You're giving up on me already?"

"Not on you," he said. "I can hunt up contracts and write your promo material. Bubbles Marlowe, Cyborg Detective—"

"Forget the cyborg thing, Dick. I can't even figure out how to use this thing. If I survive this job, we'll talk about future work. Something less punchy. Rescuing SmartPets from storm drains, maybe."

Dickie looked sideways at me. "Have you ever been in a HoloCity storm drain?"

Long streaks of neon light slid past the tinted windows of the car like someone had dragged their fingers through an oil painting. "No. Have you?"

"I heard there're alligators."

"That's just something your mother told you to keep you from getting your dress shoes soggy."

"I wouldn't go down there."

"Okay," I said. "Well, you think of something. Low-key jobs the brass doesn't care about. No more of these gamblers and hustlers and HoloCity highbinders. They play a little rough."

Dickie dropped me out front of my apartment, but he didn't come up. After nearly losing his boiler to Hawkins, he wasn't in a hurry to leave it unattended in my neighbourhood. Probably the first good idea he'd had all day. I wasn't sure how long I'd been out, but I guessed it was after noon when I pushed open the broken door into my flat and tossed my new, black trench coat and fedora on top of the fuzzy pink monstrosity on the chair. The curtains were drawn against the dreary mid-day grey outside, and the apartment swam in shadows I couldn't be bothered to dispel. Mittens didn't make an appearance. Typical cat. I should have saved myself some money and got a real one if the SmartPet was just going to ignore me anyway.

I flicked on a dim light in the kitchen and opened the fridge. No takeout containers for me. Just three cans of NRG soda and a can of pseudo-sausage product that I didn't remember opening. I grabbed a soda and held the can on my jaw until it stopped throbbing. In the corner of the kitchen, next to the recycling chute, the broom cupboard hung open a crack. An ancient sweeper bot peeked out, knocked from its charging cradle. The sweeper irritated Mittens with its refusal to accept updates, and I'd found it easier to leave it in the cupboard rather than provoke the ire of the rampaging SmartPet. I vaguely wondered when the last time my floor had been cleaned. I cracked the tab on the can and took a swig. The air in the apartment smelled different from when I'd left. I didn't think it was the mystery meat in the refrigerator. It was an animal kind of smell, low and musky.

I kicked the fridge closed and turned back to the living room. A shadowed figure stood in the far corner, beyond the reach of the dim glow from the kitchen light. It moved slightly. Something glinted in the darkness. There was a click. An icy kiss brushed the back of my neck and a harsh voice whispered, "Touch the ceiling, baby."

The shadow didn't move. It just waited. Waited while I lifted my hands up, while I spun the can so it wouldn't drip on my head, and reached. The voice said, "Good girl."

The cold, hard finger of the gun barrel trembled against my skin, and I felt the man step closer. Felt his heart beating in the space between us. He might have had a gun in his hand but he carried all his excitement in his front pocket. Hot, musky breath wafted over my shoulder. I kept my eyes on the shadow.

"I didn't realize I had company," I said. "Can I help you, gentlemen?"

"You don't look like you're in any position to help anyone," the shadow said in a feminine voice, like liquid smoke.

"Pardon me," I said. "Only one gentleman in the house."

"Oh, Dex is rarely gentle," the woman said. She leaned forward just enough so I could see the tip of her nose illuminated in the yellow glow from the kitchen, and below that a set of slightly crooked teeth between thin, red lips.

The gun man shivered again, and I hoped I wasn't going to have to do laundry after he was finished with his tough guy act. I said, "What do you want?"

"I'm just here to drop a hint," the woman said. "And to see if you're the kind of woman who knows how to pick one up."

"What kind of hint?"

"Lay off the Bell girl," the woman said. "And we can all be friends."

"Great," I said, feeling a little dread creeping up my spine next to Dex's mojo. "I can do that. Who's the Bell girl?"

The woman tsked and stood, stepping out of the shadow completely to reveal a long, narrow frame in a tightly wrapped coat like a thin, black cigarette. Long, bare legs emerged from the bottom of the jacket and made me wonder what she was wearing underneath. A thin, red scarf cut the white flesh of her slender neck. Black shoes with skyscraper heels scratched marks in the dust on my floor. She wore a little hat perched at an unnatural angle on her white-blonde hair, and in her hand, she held a pistol with barrel almost as skinny as she was. She said, "Perhaps you ought to get your memory fixed along with your door."

"That's an idea," I said. "But what's your interest in the matter?"

"We're just here to deliver a message," she said, her voice hardened, and her pale eyes peered over my shoulder at the gunman. "Isn't that right, Dex?"

Dex shifted his weight behind me, and for a fraction of a second the gun wavered from the back of my neck. I dropped my elbow into his gut and heard the wind explode from his lungs. I reached back, grabbed his wrist, and twisted so that the barrel of the gun dug into his shoulder blades. The NRG drink pooled in an electric green puddle at our feet. I pushed him in front of me like a human shield and crouched behind him. His pink scalp glistened beneath the thin, closely shaved, white-blonde hair, just like the woman's. She held the gun in our direction with the steady arm of a pro.

"I can shoot, you know," she said breathlessly. "Would you like to try me?"

"I guessed as much with a small bore like that," I said. "I'd rather you didn't. And I bet junior here feels the same."

"Should have kept your hand out of your pants," she hissed at her partner. He flinched, and I ducked a little lower, in case she decided she didn't mind dropping him to get to me. But then she laughed. A cheerful little tune like the shearing of metal. "My brother gets a little over-excited at times."

"What's the deal with the Bell girl?" I said. "Who is she to you?"

She kept the gun trained on me and sidled toward the door. "You are testing my patience."

"Know a guy by the name of Bobby Mook?"

"Maybe I do," she said. "Maybe I don't. I know a lot of guys. I didn't come here to talk about them. I came to deliver a message, and I think you heard me the first time."

I kicked the would-be gunman toward his sister, but I hung onto the gun and made sure I covered her with it.

She laughed again. "It's not loaded. I never let him carry a loaded gun."

"That rates with me," I said. "I prefer them that way."

"I heard about your accident." She smiled ruthlessly. "Lucky vetch. Not many people in this city can afford an upgrade like you've got. By the look of this pinch hole you live in, you can't either. Maybe you have well-connected friends, but they won't be enough to save you if you don't lay off the girl."

"I'll keep it in mind." I tossed the gun on the floor and kicked it toward her. "Now take your kid brother and drift."

She grabbed him by the scruff of the neck like a naughty puppy and shoved him into the hallway. Then she bent her knees to pick up the piece between her feet, keeping the slim black barrel of her gun pointed at my left eye. I didn't doubt she could hit it if she wanted to. She backed out of the door after him, and I waited until she was out of sight before I slammed it behind her.

"Thanks for dropping in," I muttered and then said to the apartment, "Alright, scaredy cat. You can come out now."

Mittens pranced into the living room on its little white feet. "Took you long enough."

"You were a big help," I said and went into the kitchen to clean up the mess left by my spilled NRG drink. "Can I run the sweeper bot, or are you going to have a conniption fit?"

"Do whatever you like with that ... thing." Mittens licked one of its nanoparticled paws and narrowed its yellow eyes at me. "I suggest the recycling chute."

I pulled open the closet where Dex must have been hiding and rummaged around until I found the sweeper. A scorch mark seared one side of the circular bot, and broken wires protruded from the bottom like multi-coloured intestines.

I dropped the bot in disgust. "You should consider charging for your services. I know a few sweethearts who'd be happy to hire you."

"I don't know what you're talking about." The cat crept toward the bot and batted at its wire guts. "Maybe you have a rat problem."

"I'm sure I do."

"Does this mean I can order a new sweeper bot?" Mittens licked its little white fangs with delicate disinterest. "Happy Bots Supply House is having a 2-for-1 deal. You could get the NutriJuicer too."

"Careful, Mittens," I said. "It almost sounds like you care about me."

"Your last biometrics got red flagged for a severely unbalanced nutritional profile," Mittens said. "You're making me look bad."

"Can we afford it?" I picked the can up and tossed it down the chute, then used a damp rag to clean up the analogue way. When I was done, I opened the fridge and took out another can of NRG.

Mittens eyed the drink skeptically. "Can you afford not to? There's more to good health than just not drinking, you know."

I took my drink into the living room and slumped into the lopsided chair. "I'll start investing in my long-term health once I'm convinced sobriety isn't going to kill me."

Mittens padded over and put its little, white paws on my knee. I bent forward and picked up the spherical bot beneath the nanoskin and placed the SmartPet on my lap. It purred and nuzzled under my chin, tickling me with its whiskers. "I do care about you, you know."

"You're just saying that so I don't sell you on the hock market."

Mittens bared its little white teeth at me. Maybe it was supposed to be a smile, but I hadn't paid for the upgraded emo-emulator, so it looked more like the cat wanted to bite me. "I intercepted a call while you were talking to your friends."

"Who from?"

"I don't know," Mittens said. "Why don't you ask? He's still holding."

I cursed and pushed the cat off my lap. Holding up my tattler, I opened the call menu and cursed again. I pushed a button and projected the glowering face of Wallace Flint onto the stained wall of my apartment. He glared at me like a vulture assessing a piece of meat deemed too rotten even for his questionable taste.

"I do not appreciate being kept waiting."

I took a swig of my soda and glared right back at him. "There's a lot of things I don't appreciate. Two of them just left, and another one is taking up too much space in my living room."

Flint eyed the room with disdain bordering on disgust dripping from his features. "I don't know that one could call this living."

"Maybe you've got a better idea about it," I said. "What with all the cush you're swimming in. Did you ever manage to pay my retainer, or did that little detail slip your mind? Kinda like the little detail about the heavies that might be interested in chewing me out over my interest in your daughter."

"What are you talking about?"

"I met the angel in question," I said. "She gave me a sore jaw. But I had it coming. It's been a few days since somebody hit me. What I don't like is having my apartment broken into on account of some high-tech lowlife who doesn't like to do his own dirty work."

"You saw Angelica?" he said. "Where?"

"In Miss Martinez's apartment," I said. "Slumming it up in the Heights. You sure the dame has her hooks in Angelica, or is it the other way around?"

"The Heights?" His face reddened, and he began to look a bit more like a turkey than a vulture.

"That's very interesting. I can assure you that Miss Martinez is after Angelica's inheritance. Vector probably has his reasons for putting her up in a place like that, but she doesn't have any money of her own. I know that much."

"What exactly are you calling for, Mr. Flint?"

Flint's lips tightened and he cleared his throat. "Actually, I—well ... The fact is I called to apologize for my behaviour earlier. I feel we got off on the wrong foot."

"Do you have a right foot? Or are you just hopping around on the wrong one until you get tired and fall down?"

"Alright," he said stiffly. "I deserve that. I've been told I'm not very personable."

"That might not be the worst thing I've heard about you."

The redness deepened and the growl came back into his voice. "You listen here, Marlowe. I'm paying good money to—"

"Are you?" I yawned. "When is that again?"

Flint jabbed at something off screen and my tattler pinged. "Fine. There you are. Your retainer is paid. Can you afford some manners now?"

"Manners don't come cheap in the Grit, Mr. Flint," I said. "But I thank you all the same. Now do you know anything about the thugs who just tried to rough me up over 'the Bell girl' as they call her? I don't see why this case should get so tough if all I'm doing is smearing the red broad with her own lipstick."

"Thugs?" he sounded shocked. "Perhaps you had better come over to discuss matters. This is getting out of hand. I'll send my car for you. Can you come immediately?"

"Sure," I said. "But I can get there on my own."

"Nonsense. I'll send my driver for you. Her name is Constance. You may rely upon her absolutely. Expect her within the hour."

I yawned again and wondered if I could catch a nap before the chauffeur made her debut. "Okay. Have her call up and I'll come down. She won't want to leave her car unattended in this neighbourhood."

I hung up and lay back in the chair, wondering if this was the line Flint used on all the ladies. Mittens insisted on being picked up again. I set the SmartPet on my chest, turned its purring module to a relaxation frequency, and took a nap.

Chapter Seven

WHEN I GOT THE call, I headed downstairs and was surprised to see the relentless grey glare of the sky had dulled to a charcoal-stained smear above the glittering black towers of the HoloCity skyline. Either Flint's driver got lost or our visit wasn't quite as high priority as Flint has pretended it was. But the nap had done me good and the rain was holding off. It was as nice an evening as we saw in the Grit.

"Ms. Marlowe?" A small, hard-looking woman stepped out of the lengthening shadows next to my building. She had sun-browned skin and cropped, grey hair and the grim expression of a street soldier.

"Yeah," I said. "You brought a boiler car?"

She tipped her head toward the alley where a slick grey machine hovered silently like an animal waiting for a chance to strike. She opened the passenger door for me and said, "Don't ding it. It's new."

"I thought Flint spent his last credits buying off the Trade Zone R&D team for the honour of their consideration," I said. "Looks like he let a few chips slip through the cracks."

"Mr. Flint doesn't mind spending money where it counts," the driver said, and slipped into the front seat. "Get in. And this car is off-grid. I don't want any distractions while I'm driving."

I shut my mouth and climbed into the boiler. The off-grid model had a lot more bells and whistles than Dickie's high-tech auto-driver. It made me a little nervous to be in a human driven vehicle. Too many variables. Too many things to go wrong. But as Constance zipped in and out of grid traffic, dropped wheels to take the machine off the maglev tracks, and generally kept us off the radar of HCPD and TZ scanners, I could see the appeal.

Constance drove us into an area of the city I wasn't familiar with. Low-slung concrete buildings spread over landscaped steppes in an imitation of an archaic adobe village. No visible tech marred the illusion. Constance dimmed the lights on the boiler car and weaved her way onto a dark-grey street. Little light from the evening sky seeped in between the buildings as we glided from shadow to shadow.

I leaned forward and spoke next to the driver's ear. "What is this place?"

"They call it the Bricks," she said. "Don't let the low-tech appearances fool you. These Luddites are drenched in cush. It's not cheap to stay off the grid."

"Tell that to the Grit skids."

"Being a pinch doesn't keep you from being watched." Constance gritted her teeth and a muscle pulsed in her jaw. We pulled up to a moulded concrete wall with a metal gate out front. The letters E.B. swirled across a crest in the centre. "Here we are."

"E.B.?"

"Evangeline Bell," she said without a trace of feeling. "Flint's dead wife. She was queen of low-tech luxury. A member of the Mezzanine Rose and everything."

"The Last Humanist cult?" I sat back and pondered that. The Last Humanists forbade the use of cybernetic enhancements, medical or recreational, as they interfered with the Absolute Purity of the human mind and body. "I guess Angelica didn't take to the programming, huh?"

"Angelica has always been a bit of a—" Constance's shoulders stiffened and her hands gripped the control wheel. "What is this?"

The car swung onto Flint's private drive just as two figures emerged from the shadows with guns drawn. I heard a voice I could have done without hearing.

"Hands up, ladies!" The words trembled out of Dex's mouth like he had something to be excited about. "This is a heist. Get out and line up against the car. I'm gonna frisk ya."

Constance's eyes slid toward me and then back toward the pink faced lunatic waving a gun around.

"If I know this guy, the thing's not loaded," I said under my breath.

Constance nodded.

"Get out the car!" Spittle flew through the air, illuminated by the low, amber light of an old-fashioned street lamp. I pushed my door open slowly.

Constance burst out on the opposite side and planted herself with her arms stretched across the roof. A pistol designed for the casual boar hunter was gripped in her steady hands.

"You asked for it," Dex shouted, and I dropped behind the open door just as a burst of flame burst out of the end of his gun. The passenger side window burst with a crash. The tinkle of falling glass landed on the pavement like rain.

I guessed he'd found some ammunition.

A crack like the sound of a bangtail breaking the sound barrier split through the quiet night, and Dex dropped to the ground with the top of his blond head opened up. He landed with one arm twisted underneath his body and a lump straining at the front of his pants. His brains sprayed out behind him on the damp, black pavement.

Footsteps thudded away from the car, and I guessed the woman in the black cigarette coat wasn't sticking around to pick up the pieces. Constance didn't give chase. She inspected the window and cursed under her breath.

"Flint's not going to like this."

I stood up and wiped the sweat off my forehead with my flesh arm. My upgrade seized against my leg as I tried to relax my muscles.

"Nice shot," I said.

"Who says it was me?"

"I didn't bring a gun to this little party," I said. "You always carry a big-game cannon like that?"

"Never hurts to be prepared," she said. "They must have been after Miss Bell."

"Why do you say that?"

"It's Thursday night," she said. "I'm usually ferrying her ass back from the clubs right about now, on the glow-down after a full day of drinking and losing money."

We went over to the body and poked around a bit. There was nothing much to see unless you like blood and grey matter. I said, "Kill those lights. Let's get out of here."

"But Mr. Flint is expecting you."

"You think Flint is going to want to keep you around after you just blew a guy's top off?" I said. "No police. He was very explicit about that. Take me back to my place. We'll get our stories straight and try again."

She appraised me coolly and put the hand cannon back in a holster hidden beneath her leather jacket. "All right. I get it. You got anything to drink?"

"No," I said. My throat tightened and a trickle of sweat ran down my back. "And I picked a damned fine time to quit."

She smacked the hood of the boiler and cursed again. "Brand-new car too. Punks like that really grind me."

"Yeah, well, you ground a couple of inches off that one," I said. "I think we can call it even."

She got in the car and slammed the door. I got in behind her. She said, "We'll see if Mr. Flint agrees."

We picked up Barbeque Tacos from Fusion Confusion on the way back to my place. The ostensible beef looked almost like animal protein, and the tacos even had a few vegetables that might have once seen natural light. Mittens would be proud. But when we got up to the apartment, the cat was hiding out in my bedroom.

Constance had parked the car in the alley behind my building, insisting that its internal defence systems were up to anything the Grit could throw at it. I wondered how she'd feel about a Molotov-cocktail thrown in through the busted window, but I didn't bother to say anything.

Sitting on the floor of my apartment with the takeout containers between us, I didn't have much of an appetite. I never did get used to dead bodies, and this was two in one day. Constance dug in heartily.

"Nice place you got here," she said through a mouthful of maybe-meat. The funny thing is, she seemed almost serious.

I snorted. "Compared to what?"

"Compared to nothing." She shrugged. "Not everybody has a place of their own."

"You live with Flint at the funny farm full time?"

"For years." She wiped her mouth with a recycled cardboard napkin with flecks of green in it.

"What's the deal with Angelica Bell?"

"There is no deal," Constance said. "She's a spoiled, rich brat who wasn't happy enough spending her daddy's money, so she had to start dipping into the inheritance that isn't hers yet."

"How long has she been going out gambling on Thursday nights?"

"Since as long as she could pass a fake ID" The woman crumpled up the napkin and tossed it on top of her empty taco wrapper. She ran a hand over her cropped grey hair and looked me in the eye. "Who do you figure for the job tonight?"

"I don't figure anything," I said. "This whole operation is upside down. Tell me about the girl."

"What do you want to know? She's a punk. Drinks heavy, likes to gamble and fool around with women of easy virtue."

"Violent?"

"Not as such." She leaned back on her elbows and gave me a hard stare. "She gave you the lump?"

"She had a little help," I said. "What about Flint?"

"You've met him."

"Does he have any money?" I took a bite of my taco. Hunger won over the queasies and I took another bite. "Or is it all his old lady's?"

"Who knows," she laughed a little, low in her throat. "The guy's so tight he needs a straw to help him take dump."

"What a way to talk about your boss."

She shrugged and said again, "You've met him."

"You really think those gunnies were waiting for Miss Bell?"

"Makes enough sense to me. She keeps a pretty regular schedule and has a habit of pissing off the wrong kind of mugs."

"She in tonight?"

"Sure," Constance said. "Wanted to sleep off a hangover instead of throwing in the chips tonight. Not the first time."

"You know why Flint hired me?"

She nodded slightly. "I hear things."

"So, what do you think's to be gained for a couple of thugs jumping Miss Bell's ride?"

"The set up is pretty obvious, isn't it?" She looked at the stubby fingernails on her left hand and inspected a hangnail. "Probably didn't mean to kill anyone. Just wanted to put the scare in her. But that punk was a loose cannon."

"I don't know Mick Vector personally," I said. "But I've met some of his associates. Those cock-ups don't fit the bill."

"Maybe that's why he picked them."

"Clever broad, huh?" I tossed in my napkin and chewed the last of my meal. "You sure you don't do some dick work on the side?"

She raised a silver eyebrow at me.

"I think you and I can get along," I said. "But what are we going to do about the stiff on your boss' drive?"

"Nothing."

"Okay. You can get rid of the gun, right? Are there cameras on the place?"

"I'll take care of it."

"You'd better. No police," I said, and my tattler rang.

Wallace Flint's beady little eyes blinked at me from the hologram. "Taking your time, aren't you, Marlowe? Or did Constance get lost trying to find your hovel?"

"We ran into a little trouble, Mr. Flint. Constance can tell you all about it."

"You listen to me, you so-called detective." He sniffed and seemed to wonder what exactly it was he wanted me to listen to. "I'm the kind of man who is used to a certain—"

"I've had a rough day, Mr. Flint. Your daughter and her girlfriend clobbered me from both sides, and not in the fun way. Then I find a couple of thugs waiting for me in my apartment, telling me to lay off the Bell girl. And now—"

Constance shook her head slightly and I stopped.

"Forgive me for not being more sympathetic, Marlowe," Flint said loud enough to make the tattler's speakers crackle. "But I did pay you for a particular job to be done."

"If you don't like the way I operate," I said. "You can find someone else to do the job. But with the bodies piling up, you might have a tough time finding anyone to take it. Did you get a visit from the boys in grey this evening?"

"Grey?" Flint's voice soured. "You mean police?"

"You know the ones," I said. "We were trying not to arouse their interest."

"Why should I have gotten a visit?" He bobbed his birdlike head in my direction, turned it slightly to one side and blinked furiously.

"There's a dead man on your driveway, Mr. Flint," I said. "Most of him, anyway. I suppose some of him might have ended up on your fence. He's missing the top half of his head."

Stunned silence made the tattler whine. "Excuse me?"

"He took a shot at Constance and I. Must have recognized the car. Probably he was waiting for the return of your angel. Now what do you think of that?"

"That's ridiculous," he said. "How can a dead man take a shot at anyone, I—"

"Maybe I ought to let Constance explain to you," I said. "Maybe you're in shock."

"You get in that car and get over here at once!" The tattler really screamed with him this time. I took the volume down a notch. His face purpled with rage. "Do you hear me? On the double!"

"Constance will tell you," I said softly, and killed the call.

Constance licked her teeth and stuffed the takeout wrappers inside the box we'd carried them in. She said, "Thanks for that. I thought we were making a plan."

"It's his driveway," I said. "He's got to decide if he's in it with the rest of us or if he's just going to stand around on the sidelines and promise to throw some money at us."

"Save it," she said. "I'll see myself out. Good luck with Miss Bell."

She slammed the door behind her and stomped down the hallway. I picked up the remains of our meal and stuffed them into the appropriate disposal chutes. Most of it was trash. The tacos churned in my belly, and I rested my head over the sink until the feeling passed. Something about this job stank. I didn't think my guts would feel any better until I uncovered the offending nugget and dealt with it appropriately.

Footsteps pounded up to my door again. I leaned against the counter and flexed the fingers of my upgrade, wishing I had kept Dex's gun. Maybe all this could have been avoided if I had. Someone banged on the door. I had a feeling it wasn't Constance. Maybe the slim blonde was coming back to have a chat about her brother.

I strode over to the door, put my flesh hand on the doorknob, and cocked my metal fist up by my head in case I needed to hit someone and get away quickly. I twisted the handle slowly. Too slowly for the heavy on the other side. The door slammed into my boot where I braced against the attack.

A familiar voice shouted, "Open up, Bubbles. I know you're in there."

No police, they said. Completely off Swain's radar, they said. I groaned and opened the door the rest of the way. "You don't give a girl much of a chance to get presentable, do you, Detective Weiland?"

"By 'get presentable' do you mean 'destroy the evidence'?" The big man shoved his way into my tiny apartment, seeming to suck all the air out of it as he went. His partner, a skinny slimeball I remembered as Clive Harold, slithered in after him and looked around my flat with half-lidded eyes and a self-satisfied smirk.

"Would I tell you if I did?"

Harold picked up my jacket from the chair and started going through the pockets. "Sounds guilty to me."

"You think the law applies any less to me because I used to be one of you?" I yanked the jacked from his hands and pushed passed him into the kitchen just so I could have a little breathing room. The boys followed.

"You remember Harold, don't you, Bubbles?" Weiland opened my fridge, looked inside, and shook his head sadly.

"Get your paws off my stuff, Tom," I said. "This isn't a social call."

Weiland glowered at me with muddy grey eyes that matched his uniform. He crossed his arms and looked at his new partner.

"I hear you used to be a pretty good shot," Harold said, and leaned against the counter and picked his teeth with a long pinky nail.

"Depends on the kind of shot you're looking for," I said, and threw Weiland a look that said he'd get what was coming to him if he'd been flapping his lips about me.

Harold pointed at me with a finger and mimed pulling the trigger. "A good shot."

I dug in my pocket for a piece of gum and made a big show of unwrapping it and putting it in my mouth. I chewed with exaggerated slowness until Weiland finally cracked.

"Look, Bubbles," he said. "Who do you know up in the low-tech compound? The Bricks? That's not your scene."

"What do you know?" I turned on him. "You didn't want to listen to me when we were partners. Maybe I talked about the Bricks all the time while you were busy polishing up the old career?"

Harold snickered and Weiland's face went pale. "I said I was sorry about that, Bubbles. You know—"

"No, Tom. I don't know. I don't know a damn thing about anything. Never did, and I certainly don't now. Why this interest in the Bricks? What's it got to do with me?"

"You been out tonight?"

"Sure. In and out. You know how it is. You used to, anyway."

Weiland's jaw clenched and through his teeth he said, "Who did you see?"

"That's none of your business, 'partner.' My clients have a right to their privacy."

"What clients?" Weiland swelled to twice his already considerable size. I worried he might pop before he worked up the guts to ask me what he really wanted to ask me. "Damn it, Bubbles. I'm trying to help you."

"No, Tom. You aren't trying to help me. You're trying to help your career and I just happened to get in your way. Now, is one of you goofs going to tell me what this is about, or do I have to wait for the phony papers to be filed?"

Harold put up his hands and slid between Detective Weiland and me. He sidled into the living room and made a hack job of searching the place without searching. Weiland and I had a stare off in the kitchen. Harold glanced back at us a couple times, made sure we were still busy, and started sidling his way toward the hallway and my bedroom.

"You seem to know your way around pretty well, Detective Harold." I kept my eyes on Weiland to gauge his reaction. "You been here before?"

Harold sneered. Even in the haze of my peripheral vision I could see the jagged, rat-like teeth in his skinny face. He came back to the kitchen and said, "Since lover boy here isn't going to tell you, I will. We got a call tonight. About a body up in the Bricks."

"You keep harping on about the Bricks," I said. "Didn't you hear Weiland? That's not my scene."

"We wouldn't have pegged you for it," he said. "Last the department's heard, you were holed up after the accident, drinking yourself into an early grave."

"Sorry to disappoint you."

Harold ran the long nail on his pinky finger along his teeth, making a click-click-click noise like a stick dragged across a chain-link fence. "Then we got another call."

"You get a lot of calls." I pushed Weiland out of my way and grabbed my last can of NRG out of the fridge. "Must be nice."

"This caller said if we want to know about the body in the Bricks, we should talk to a Betty 'Bubbles' Marlowe who lives in a skid-hole apartment in the old industrial zone and keeps her nose a little too clean to be honest."

"Now, now"—I cracked the tab on my drink—"you embellished that last part. Nobody ever accused me of keeping my nose clean. That's how I had my little 'accident.'"

Weiland rubbed his face with his big hands until the skin became raw and pink. His eyes looked bleary and the bags beneath them had thin, purple veins tracing away from them. "It was an accident, Bubbles."

"Keep telling yourself that, if it helps you sleep at night." I finished the drink and crushed the can in my cybernetic fist. For once, it did exactly what I wanted it to. The detectives flinched at the noise and their eyes landed on the upgrade as if for the first time. I said, "But by the looks of it, you need a new mantra."

"How's about you tell us what you know about the stiff out front of the Bell place," Harold said. He licked his lips with a wet, red tongue. They glistened with a thick layer of saliva that sprayed when he spoke. "And then you can show us the papers on that piece you're wearing."

"That's not what we're here for, Harold." Weiland looked like he had finally figured something out that wasn't spoon fed to him from the brass.

"The hell it isn't," the rat-faced man said through his teeth. A fine mist exploded into the air between us.

I stepped back. "Sounds like a nice tip. A little too nice if you ask me."

"All right, Bubbles. Here it is. We got a no-name phone call pointing us in the direction of the Bricks, and we find a skinny guy in a bad suit missing most of his hair and part of his brains, all laid out across the driveway of the deceased Last Humanist philanthropist, Evangeline Bell. The husband, Wallace Flint, is a big-time tech developer for Libra. Rarely leaves the lab. Nobody in the house saw or heard anything—not even the disgruntled maintenance staff, and there were a few of them. The consensus is that Flint's big on brains and low on social skills. We ID'd the stiff as a Dexter Wagner. Small-time grifter, as far as we can tell, no history of violence but a little on the wacky side. Flint wouldn't use a guy like that to clean his toilets, so that angle is out. They don't use cameras up in the Bricks, so we got no leads there. The hole in his head looks like it was carved out by a cannon ball. Then we get this other call that says if we want to know about the stiff, we should ask you. So here we are. Asking."

"This is your asking?" I stuffed the crushed can into the recycling chute and leaned on the counter. "Well this is my telling. I don't own a gun. I haven't fired a gun since my service rifle blew up. Can't stomach them."

"Okay," Weiland said. "Now we're getting somewhere."

"You buying this trash?" Harold spat the words. "I want a trace scan. You give me a trace scan that proves you ain't got no residuals on you, and I'll happily remove myself from this flea-bitten skid hole. Without a scan, these are just words. The words of a person known to the department to be deceitful and self-serving."

"Yeah," I said. "I got served up real nice." Turning to Weiland, I said, "Is this guy for real?"

"Let me scan you and we'll leave," Weiland said.

"You'll leave," I said. "All right. It doesn't rate, but I'm tired and I want to be able to sleep without hissy over here spitting all over me. You do it."

Weiland did a surface bio-sweep using a small, handheld scanner. There were smaller, cybernetic versions on the black market. Rae had offered to install one in my upgrade. But HCPD weren't allowed to have any internal tech ever since a hacking incident thirty-some years ago turned HoloCity into a war zone with enhanced police officers and district kings attacking anything that moved. The brass still viewed cybernetic enhancements with a mixture of fear and envy. I could see Harold's throat working as he watched Weiland scan the arm, his eyes darting back and forth beneath saggy eyelids.

"She's clean," Weiland said.

Harold threw his arms up in disgust and said, "I'm going down to the patrol car. Get her papers. And don't linger, lover boy, or I'm taking this higher up the chain."

The skinny man slammed his way out the door and stomped along the hallway. Weiland sagged with relief. He said, "Thank you."

"I'm serious, Tom. I've had a long day and I want to go to sleep."

"How have you been?" He looked me hard in the eye, studying my face without blinking.

"You're lingering," I said. "That's bad for you career, and for my reputation."

His jaw clenched again and he looked away. Then he moved his bulk slowly toward the door. A pang like regret hit me right between the ribs. Probably indigestion from the pseudo-beef tacos. He opened the door and put a hand on the jamb. He paused like he wanted to say something. I wanted him to say it, and I didn't. I held my breath.

He said, "You know a guy named Bobby Mook?"

"Not your best line," I said, trying to cover my disappointment.

"Listen," Tom said. "A little guy, one of Vector's bookies. You ever heard of him?"

"Nothing of interest," I said. "But if he's one of Vector's he's probably got more than one trick up his sleeve."

"He's got a couple of new buttons on his vest," Weiland said. "Lead ones. Little target buttons. Right over the heart. You know anyone who likes a small bore?"

"Not many guys on the street have that kind of finesse."

"That was my line of thinking."

I said, "You're still lingering."

"Okay," he said.

He closed the door gently behind him. I barely heard his footsteps as they disappeared down the hallway, but I pressed my forehead against the door and listened anyway. For the second time that day, tears stung my eyes. At least this time, there was no one there to see me cry.

Chapter Eight

I DIDN'T SLEEP. I sat on my wonky chair and sulked. Mittens came out of hiding and sat with me for a while. Then the cat said, "I recorded it. Just in case."

"Thanks." I wiped the back of my hand over my eyes and pushed my bangs out of my face. "Not that anyone would care if they'd gotten rough."

"Maybe not," Mittens said. "But the feedreels love that kind of stuff. It might be enough to make the Chief uncomfortable."

"Last time I made Swain uncomfortable, he returned the favour."

"You didn't have the media behind you that time. You have to think about things differently now. You aren't on the force. They don't like you. But that opens other avenues of protection. Like this guy Vector that just called."

"Mick Vector?"

"I intercepted that one too." Mittens purred and rolled over to expose its belly. "Figured the uniforms were giving you a hard enough time without that angle. He left a message for you."

I tickled the nanoparticle fur absently. "What message?"

"Wants to meet you at the Heights," it said. "To talk business."

"Great. You know he's the one behind the shill I'm supposed to smear for Flint, right?"

"Doesn't hurt to keep your options open," Mittens said and grabbed my hand with its claws. "You don't even like Flint."

"I like Rae." I shook the tingling sensation out of my hand and glared at the SmartPet. "And I don't like Vector's methods."

Mittens shrugged in a way no real cat ever could. "Want to call him back?"

"I'll go," I said. "Might as well spend a bit of this retainer before I get myself faded."

"You want a ScanAnon pass? You can afford it."

"Nah," I said. "Let them watch me if they want to. I don't feel like hiding anymore."

"It's your funeral."

I set the cat on the floor and pulled on the overcoat and hat I'd gotten from Dickie. "Do I still look like a pro skirt?"

"Maybe one that doubles as a hitman."

"Close enough," I said, and called in the ride.

I had to hoof it a ways to the nearest pick-up point. The auto-driving hacks don't go down the tertiary roads without video surveillance on every corner. Too easy for a mob of desperate skids to overpower a slow-moving pod, knock out the maglev system, and piece it out for the hock market. I knew HCPD could be watching me. My ID would pop up in the hack system, and if I was flagged—and of course I was—someone down at headquarters would hear about it. But it was late, and the night shift was notoriously lazy, so there was a chance they wouldn't catch my movements until morning. In any case, they probably wouldn't try anything inside Gibson Heights. Even Swain watched his step around the highbinders.

So I got inside the hack pod, sat back, and let it take me back to the pretty glass dome that protected HoloCity's richest, most virtuously delicate snowflakes. The hack slid smoothly and silently along the grid, first through the Grit strips thick with crowds partaking in the night trades, then through the quieter but heavily surveilled corridors of the Biz District, where back-alley dealers kept to the shadows between towering skyscrapers. Gibson Heights sat above it all, a glittering mound of wealth in a city of deep disparity. What was I doing mixed up with people like this? The case was smelling worse with every passing moment, and somewhere in the middle of it all, I knew I'd find the worm of corruption digging beneath the surface. I closed my eyes and let my mind wander over all the little details, trying to find what I was missing.

Hawkins let me into the Heights through a man door reserved for staff. Rental hacks weren't allowed in the garages, he said. Only privately owned cars. But he'd been expecting me.

I said, "I hear Vector's in."

"Sure." His dark eyes, partially hidden behind the visilenses, slid nervously over me as he held the door open. Probably he was scanning me again, just in case. "I'll take you up."

He led me through a narrow, white corridor and filed me into a narrow, white box like the lift I'd shared with Mungo. But Hawkins didn't take up half so much space and he smelled nicer, Like the way perfume companies want us to imagine fresh running water smells like. We know it's a lie, but it hits all the same buttons in the brain anyway, so we keep buying into it. Hawkins gave a verbal code, and the room shifted almost imperceptibly. A small, orange light above the doors indicated that we were in motion and shouldn't attempt to open the doors, though they had no handles I could see. Hawkins tapped long brown fingers against a lean, muscular thigh, the pink moons of his fingernails making a soft scratching noise in the otherwise silent transporter.

When the doors opened, Hawkins led the way into the strangely luminous corridor. Shadows moved on either side of us, performing acts both lewd and banal. Hawkins didn't look at them and I didn't either. He stopped in front of Miss Martinez's suite and said his code again, then moved aside so I could pose for the cameras.

"Beat it, Hawkins," a gravelly voice said over the intercom. My chaperone narrowed his eyes and twitched his jaw a couple of times. Then he spun on his heels and stalked back toward the lift. Once he was gone, the door opened.

A barrel-chested man—not so big as he wouldn't fit through the doorway, but almost—filled the space between the frames. He leaned down to look at me a little closer. He had a soft, brown face with tawny cheeks and a wide, hooked nose. His thick black eyebrows looked like they had their own personal stylist and curved delicately up over his nose in a way that made him appear both sinister and comical.

"You must be Marlowe." He grinned at me and I stepped back, not sure what the grin meant. "What brings you to the Heights?"

"I was under the impression that I'd been summoned," I said. Then, uncertainly, I added, "Sir."

"You know who I am?"

"If you're Scarlett Martinez, your looks have taken a bit of a dive."

He leaned back and laughed heartily, his belly bouncing up and down like a balloon dancing in the wind. He said, "Come inside. Come inside."

"Is Miss Martinez in?" I stepped inside the apartment for the second time that day and noticed a different feel in the air. The scent of cloves still lingered, but the air no longer held the haze of kretek smoke. Another big man with a bigger gun leaned against the glass table where Scarlett had prepared her drink. He wore black sunglasses and turned his head so that he wasn't looking in my direction, which almost certainly meant he was.

"No." Vector seated himself in a low-slung chair that looked like a melting meringue. "She told me you'd been bothering her, though. Asked me to have a chat with you about some of your stranger ideas."

"My ideas are strange?" I didn't sit. "Here I thought I was the only one who made any sense."

"Does working for Flint make sense?"

"Not the way he likes it," I said. "But if I can do it my way, I don't see the harm in it."

"Why are you busting Scarlett's chops?" Vector leaned forward so that his belly hung between his knees, straining the fine pearly buttons that held his silver suit jacket together. "Don't you believe in true love?"

"Not with that kind of money involved," I said.

The man's oversized eyebrows drooped in oversized sorrow. "Such a cynical heart."

"Don't twist this around on me," I said. "None of this is my idea. Now why am I here?"

"Scarlett told me something about you," he said. "Something that interests me very much. I'd like to hear your version of it."

"Forget Scarlett for a minute," I said. "Where's the Bell girl?"

"She owes me some dough. I don't keep her on a leash."

"No, but Miss Martinez does and then she brings it to you when it needs a sharp tug, is that right?"

"What exactly do you think the nature of Scarlett's work is for me?"

I clenched my teeth together, knowing that if he had to ask, I probably had everything upside down. "I know what it looks like."

"Scarlett Martinez has one of the finest unadulterated minds in HoloCity." Vector steepled his fingers before his round, moon face and leaned back in the chair. It made an inorganic squeaking noise, but it held. He watched me with dark irises encased in heavy folds of flesh so that his eyes looked like the thin hollow crescents of a mask. "She can run numbers as fast as most computers and has an eye for human ticks and tells that machines still can't replicate. If I suspect someone's trying to game the house, all I have to do is have Scarlett watch them for a hand or two and she can tell me what they are doing and how they are doing it. She is invaluable to me. So, if she happens to fall for a girl who can't hold her liquor or her holocreds, I am inclined to indulge the relationship."

"Never mind the eight mil the Bell girl is set to inherit in a few weeks."

"I will take back what she owes me," Vector said. "Not a single chip more."

"How noble."

"The thing is, Marlowe, you're thinking like a Grit skid. You can't help what you are, but you can't see the whole picture from where you are, down there in the gutter. I understand human nature. I understand that inheriting millions of cred is not going to cure the angel of her habits. I don't have to take what isn't mine. I simply have to wait for her to give it to me."

I turned my back on Vector and looked at my own reflection on the wall behind me. My pink hair hung in lank strings around my face. Black smudges darkened the shadows beneath my eyes. Fresh red scars peeked out beneath the collar of my black jacket, glistening faintly in the low, yellow light. I looked every inch a Grit skid in a class joint like this. It ground on me a bit. But worse was that he was right. This was an angle I hadn't considered.

I said, "It might interest you to know that someone tried to hold up the Bell girl's car this evening. Got himself shot in the process."

"You think I play games like that?"

I walked over to the glass serving table where the thug leaned with his gun. He didn't acknowledge my presence in the least. I reached behind him and flipped up the hidden door that opened the ice box and pulled out a bottle of lunar water. I felt Vector's eyes on me as I took out a glass and filled it with crushed ice. I poured the crystal-clear liquid out of the blue bottle and into the glass and sipped it. I leaned on the serving table next to the thug and stared back at Vector.

"I asked you a question," he said.

I took another sip and said, "I know. I'm thinking about how to answer. The short answer is no—I wouldn't have. But it happened. I was there. I saw it. I just dealt with a couple of my old pals in the HCPD to convince them that I wasn't the one who pulled the trigger. The truth is, I don't know what to think anymore."

"Let me help you to understand," he said. "Tell me about it."

"It happened in the Bricks." A trickle of condensation slipped from the glass, along my fingers, and down my wrist. "I was on my way to discuss matters with Flint."

"What matters?"

"The kind of matters I'm too myopic to understand."

"And you think I had something to do with this would-be heist? It doesn't rate."

"It doesn't look too good on you if something happens to the Bell girl when she owes you so much dough."

"That's not the way I see it." Vector rested his hands upon his generous belly and leaned back until the chair protested. "If the Bell girl dies, I'm out a hundred K stacks. I should be paying you to babysit her."

"Might be you wanted to send a message to anyone else holding out on their debts," I said. "Might be you just wanted to scare her. I don't know. It's hard to see from down here in the gutter."

He laughed his bouncing laugh again and his eyes disappeared beneath the heavy black brow. "You're sore now. Don't be sore. I like you."

"I hope no one holds it against me." I said. "Now why did you really want to see me?"

"There's another guy got himself shot up today," Vector said. "A one-time friend of mine named Bobby Mook. You went to see him after your left Libra. I know this because you had a tail."

"The guy I almost ran over outside of Glitter Haus?" I asked. "Or the old guy poking his head out of Vitality Industries?"

Vector leaned back in his chair and laughed heartily. "You are good. You are very good. One of them. Maybe both. Maybe more. It doesn't matter. This tail knows you went in to see Mook shortly after you took the job from Flint, but that you were too late to ask him any questions. You didn't call the brass. This makes me think you and I could get along just fine."

"Mook's shooting looks worse for you than anything with the Bell girl," I said. "What kind of black paint was he slinging?"

"That I don't know," Vector said. "And now it seems we won't find out."

"That's all you wanted?"

"I wanted to see Scarlett," Vector said. "But it looks like she's not coming back this evening. I have to get back to work."

The thug pushed himself off the cabinet and stood himself up next to the door. Vector heaved his bulk out of the misshapen chair and wiped some imaginary dust from the sleeves of his silver suit. He put his hands in his pockets and said, "You coming?"

"Mind if I stay and finish my drink?" I tipped my glass at him. "Not very often I get to wet my whistle with the pure stuff."

Vector's rounded shoulders shrugged. "Why not? I pay the rent. And it will annoy Hawkins."

"Thank you, sir."

"Just do me a favour and stay out of Scarlett's way." He rolled toward the door.

"Just so long as she stays out of mine."

"Stay sharp, Marlowe." Mick Vector opened the door and closed it again, leaving a big empty space where the boys had been.

I looked around the apartment again, feeling a little dizzy. Nothing fit together worth a Grit strip pinch. Vector was right. Out of everyone, he had the least motive to go after Angelica Bell. Scarlett had the means and the motive, but she was better off with Angelica alive too. At least until they were married and the inheritance came through. I poked around the room again, looking for the ideas I might have had and lost before Angelica clobbered me.

The bedroom was more or less as I'd left it this morning. A tall, hurricane-style lamp on one end table swirled with dancing bubbles and emitted a soft, yellow glow. The drawer of the end table was slightly ajar. I peeked inside, but it was empty except for a charging port. The bathroom was as simple and elegant as a woman like Scarlett might expect. A rumpled hand towel sat next to the sink that wasn't there before, so someone had been in and out since the girls left me napping under the chaise lounge.

I came out of the bathroom and looked around the bedroom again. The clove smell was still there. But there was something else, faint, like a dream you can't quite shake. It wasn't the first time I'd smelled it today. I bent down and lifted the skirt of the bed. Something glinted at me from the darkness. I reached under with my upgrade, hooked a metal finger around the thing, and pulled it out.

An elegant handgun, the kind highbinder broads favoured to go with their evening dresses, dangled from my finger as I stood up and sniffed at the barrel. The acrid stink of burned power lingered inside. Another small bore. Wake up,

HoloCity, the ladies have learned to shoot. I dropped it in the pocket of my trench coat and eyed the room for any signs of a struggle. I had an idea about who it might belong to, and for some reason, I didn't want one of our illustrious HCPD detectives finding it.

My gaze landed on the pearlescent folding door separating the clothes closet from the rest of the room. It was a delicate looking thing, designed to reflect light and attention from the mundanity within. Or I supposed that was the idea. I didn't give a gutter-rat's ass about interior design. This particular door sat a little crooked, though, and that did interest me. It interested me very much.

I pushed on the door. It stuck. I pushed harder. The slender ovular knob dug into the palm of my flesh hand and I threw my shoulder into it too. The door flexed and then broke. Its slider jumped out of the track and, unhinged, the door fell sideways and away, revealing a pile of tough looking black techwear and leather. Then the shape tumbled forward, and Angelica Bell stared up at me with two dead blue eyes and one red one right between them.

I fell backward and tripped on the corner of the bed, landing hard on my right hip. The young woman's face leered at me, and her left hand flopped over her muscular chest and pointed with blunt fingernails. An internal tattler had been torn out of her right forearm, leaving behind a reddish-brown hole and a pool of congealed blood. Her subdermal implants made her skin mottled and scaled, and somehow, more human in death than she had seemed in life. Her black hair fell across her forehead in a childish way, like she'd just woken up from a nap.

I pushed myself out of the room, crawling backwards on my hands and feet like a crab. Stood up. Checked my pocket for the gun. Then I wiped down every surface I thought I might have touched on either visit, knowing full well I'd be obliterating the biomarkers of the killer as well. I found a stairwell opposite the lift and took that rather than calling Hawkins up, and somehow managed to find my way out of the building and into the cold, rainy, HoloCity night. Outside the gate, I threw up on the grid.

A holomonitor popped out of the sidewalk and shook a finger at me. "Ah, ah, ah! Someone's had too much fun tonight. Would you like me to call a private car? SecurityFirst Chaperone Services guarantee that you will arrive at your destination safely. Complimentary medical flushes available for when you've really overindulged! Package pricing is available—"

I stumbled away from the advertisement, barely feeling my feet hit the spongy surface of the kinetic sidewalk. I closed my eyes and turned my face up to the drizzling rain as if I could wash away the job if I stood there long enough. This was bad. Very bad. Three bodies now, and all of them linked to me. Chief Swain would have a field day if Detective Weiland and his slimeball partner connected the dots. It didn't matter that I hadn't done the killing. Swain wasn't going to concern himself with details like that. It was a wonder he hadn't already pulled a handful of fake charges out of his ass and served me up with an extended holiday in the can. Probably he was biding his time, hoping to land something stickier on me in case I had friends in low places.

I did. But not the kind that could help me now.

I heard the click before I felt the cold barrel of the gun kiss the back of my neck. The chill of déjà vu crept across my shoulder blades. The last guy to pull this move was dead. Which meant—

"How about you call up a cab, sweetheart," the ice-blonde woman whispered in my ear. "We need a little privacy, don't you think?"

She jabbed something through my jacket and into my left shoulder, just above the upgrade. The metal arm seized up, curling in on itself like the leg of a rusted up robotic insect. She said, "Don't get any clever ideas."

"Sure," I said. "I never had many of them anyway."

I tested to see if the tattler still worked, then called up the hack-pod service I'd used to bring me here. We stood there in silence, her behind me with the skinny barrel of the target gun pressed into my spine. The rain found its stride, and the cold water cascaded over my face and soaked into my clothes until I was as wet as one of Dickie's sewer gators and about as mad. But when the hack pulled up, I let the blonde push me inside and I didn't make a fuss when she crawled in beside me.

The silence continued inside the hack, the drumming of the rain and the woman's soft panting breath the only sounds to be heard. Now

I could see her; her gentle coif of frosty hair had collapsed into damp waves like albino seaweed. Her thin, red lips stretched thin in her pale face and her eyes had hardened into something like iced metal, as cold and grey as early morning light. Streaks of mascara crept from the corners of her eyes toward the hair above her ears, which the rain hadn't been able to wash away.

"Get out," she said when the hack pod pulled up in front of my building. I complied and let her march me up the back stairs and to my door.

The emptiness of my flat hit me harder than it ever had before. It was a pathetic place to live. It was an even more pathetic place to die. The woman wrapped her frigid fingers around the back of my neck and pushed me into the lopsided chair by the door as the gun pressed insistently against my temples. Mittens, the little traitor, was nowhere to be seen.

"I told you to lay off the Bell girl," she whispered. "You shouldn't have been in that car."

"Easy there," I said. "You don't want to do something you'll regret."

"What makes you think I'd regret it?" She jabbed me in the side of the head and then walked around so I could see her in front of me. A narrow, red scarf wrapped around her throat like a knife wound. The thin, black jacket gaped open at the chest, revealing a white blouse gone transparent in the rain. A small pink nipple poked through beside the lapel like it was ready for a party but had shown up at the wrong address. The cigarette shaped jacket was longer than her skirt, and her pale bare legs stuck out the bottom like doll's legs, straight into a pair of heels not made for running in. She said, "You killed my brother."

"He shot at me." I searched the room behind her for some clue as to how to get out of this mess. Nothing knocked me over the head. "You said his gun wasn't loaded."

"He fooled me on that," she said, and sighed. "That's on me. I should have watched him closer. But you dropped him. He's dead."

"I didn't drop him," I said. "I don't even carry a gun."

"That so?"

She held her pistol a little sideways so that it glinted in the dim kitchen light. A clear, gel-like substance wrapped around the barrel of the gun. Some kind of organic silencer. Nobody in my building would be concerned with a little gunfire, but I appreciated the effort.

Through her thin lips, she said, "You should have laid off."

"Maybe. I can see that a little better now. I always was a slow learner."

"Not anymore," she said. "Now, are you comfortable? I'd like you to be comfortable. I don't want a lot of fuss."

Where the hell was that cat? It could call someone for me ... not the police, but Dickie maybe. Or Rae.

And then we'd probably all get shot.

Would Tom be off duty yet? He owed me. He knew I was right about Swain and he kept his big yap shut. A career man through and through.

Stupid cat.

I said, "I don't know when's the last time you looked a gun barrel in the eye, but I'm not too comfortable."

"I never did like a big emotional goodbye. Dex went nice and quick, I'll give you that. You didn't let him suffer."

"Are those big, icy greys of yours nearsighted?" I snapped. Nerves made me edgy. "I didn't shoot. The heavy in the front took care of that. She didn't even blink."

"It's a nice story," she said. "She said you'd say something like that."

"Who said?"

A thumping noise from the kitchen made her flinch, and I ducked. But she didn't fire. She didn't even turn her head. Too bad. That might have given me an angle. Another thump and then a crash as the stacks of who-knows-what I had stacked in the storage closet fell out and scattered across the kitchen floor. She glanced quickly, too quickly for me to react. Then locked her gaze on me again. A grinding sound, like nuts and bolts being chewed up in little metal teeth, came from somewhere in the middle of the mess. A dusty cardboard box lurched out of the pile and moved toward us. She wasn't watching it.

"What the—" I stared at the box, trying to figure out what was going on.

She laughed and shook her head. "Nice try."

"No, there's a ..." Words failed me. What was it? Was Mittens in there?

"Dex must have knocked something loose," she said. "You almost had me with that look on your face. Maybe you should have been an actor. Feedreels love watching people screw up their own lives."

The box crept closer. It was almost directly behind her. I said, "That's not a bad idea."

"Why don't you get up," she said through clenched teeth. Her hand trembled a little. The ice-cold broad was no cold-hearted killer, but she seemed determined to see it through. "I'd feel better if you were laying down."

"Sure," I said. I stood slowly, keeping my flesh arm up and the upgrade curled against my chest. "It's important to feel good when you're murdering innocent people."

"Shut up," she hissed. "And move."

I moved. I stepped straight toward her, slow but deliberate. Not so fast that she'd panic and shoot me, but close enough that she had to step back. The back of her bare calves connected with the box. Her jaw dropped open and her big eyes bugged. She flailed her arms once, twice. The box pushed into her calves and she toppled backward. The gun went off. I saw a little spout of fire but didn't hear anything until the bullet made a soft puff in my drywall. The box tipped over to reveal my sweeper bot, trailing wires like some kind of undead sea creature. It grinded its way toward the woman, reached out with a skinny arm, like an antennae, and zapped her.

The woman cried out. Her eyes rolled back in her head and she dropped the pistol, rolling onto her side to protect herself from whatever the little bot was juicing her with. I lunged forward and kicked the gun into the hall. I pulled the woman's arms behind her back and twisted them with one hand.

"What did you do to my arm?"

She didn't respond. I rolled her onto her chest and kept my weight on her shoulders. I quickly reached up and felt around the top of my upgrade. Something was wedged into the flesh behind the metal shoulder cap. I grabbed onto it and pulled. Pain seared across my shoulders and down my arm, and the upgrade spasmed. My eyes burned and I gritted my teeth. The arm jerked and twitched with each pulse of pain my nerves shot into me. But then it settled and the upgrade relaxed. I flexed my fingers a couple times to make sure it was working normally again. Then I pulled the scarf from the woman's neck and used it to bind her hands behind her back.

I looked at the thing that had incapacitated the upgrade, an elongated teardrop shaped needle slick with my blood. I dropped it onto the floor and crushed it beneath the heel of my boot.

"Well," said a voice from the hallway. Yellow eyes blinked at me. "That went much better than I expected it to."

I looked from Mittens to the mangled sweeper bot. "Were you ... driving that thing?"

"You said I could order a new one," the cat said. "So I decided to play with it a little before I killed it. I am a cat, after all."

"I don't think that's how cats usually play with their food."

The cat's eyes narrowed and it licked a little white paw. "You're welcome."

"What was that thing she stabbed me with?" I asked the cat. "Have you ever come across something like that?"

"Nothing chemical, but it wouldn't have to be. Your nerves and muscles control the arm. If she hit the right nerve in the right way, it might be enough to confuse the biofeedback systems."

"Great," I said. "Anti-tech acupuncture."

I kicked the bot away from the woman and checked her pulse. She blinked rapidly in my direction. And as her eyes focussed on me, she let out a stream of curses that would make a Grit District pro skirt blush.

"Cool it," I said. "You should be thanking me. You're no killer."

She started crying then, big wracking sobs that shook her whole body. She glared up at me through a stream of tears, and her red mouth twisted away from her teeth in a look of pure despair. "Why did you have to do it? Why did you have to kill Dex?"

"I didn't kill your brother," I said. "It was Flint's supposed chauffer. Constance. You know her? What made you show up then, I'd like to know. Who were you trying to give the shake to?"

She pressed her lips closed tight and shook her head.

"I don't suppose you know a little flake called Bobby Mook, do you?" I bent to wipe her hair from her forehead. "The guy got shot with a small bore like yours sometime this morning. Maybe it's yesterday morning now."

She shook her head again.

"Who hired you to kill the Bell girl?"

Her eyes got wide and she sniffed. "That wasn't in the contract."

"You just wanted to put a scare on her?"

She closed her mouth and turned her head away from me.

"Fine," I said. "You can tell your story to my friend Detective Weiland. He'll be decent enough to you."

Mittens padded over to the woman and batted at the sole of her shoe with its paw. "You're going to give him a cookie after what he did to you?"

"Put the call in," I said. "But give me a half hour head start. I have to deliver some bad news to Mr. Wallace Flint."

I picked up the woman's gun and stuffed it in the icebox. "You know, someone's gone to some effort to make stiffs with small bullets in them. If I were you, that'd make me a little sore."

I felt the pocket of my jacket. The gun from Miss Martinez's apartment was still there. One more tick in the "enthusiastic amateur" box for the icy blonde. She cursed me one more time before I slammed the door and headed down the threadbare stairs and out into the rain.

Chapter Nine

I CALLED DICKIE ON my way down and told him what I needed. He was half asleep and drooling in his shoes but managed to catch the drift after a couple of flybys. I felt a little guilty about waking him after the rough morning we'd had, but I couldn't afford to have HCPD track me to the Bricks.

I needed to talk to Flint. Alone.

I didn't feel like standing around, so I had Dickie pick me up in front of my old drinking and dancing haunt, techRose. I hoofed it from the old industrial wasteland toward the dirty neon and misty holograms of the strip. As soon as I got there, though, I regretted it. It came at me like a long-forgotten dream, or a nightmare. Bodies clothed in more sequins and glitter than actual clothing huddled beneath the scattered awnings along the Grit's famous clubbing zone. The pinches and drunks were out in full force, stumbling out of blackened doorways, crouched in the narrow corridors between multi-level party houses, puking in the gutters. The rain came down. It didn't make a dent in the filth.

Standing outside techRose, with the bass from the music inside thumping out into the streets and the laughter of streetwise girls and boys getting their glow on, I felt my throat constrict and the muscles in my chest tighten. The rain and the glitter and the lights, the smell of street cart food wafting out from beneath kaleidoscopic awnings. It made me hungry; hungry for the life I'd left behind, willingly or not. There was a hole inside my soul that had been scraped out, slowly, after years of filling it up with this place. I had been washed away from the inside out, like the caves left behind by an underground river. Now that fluid life force had dried up, and I was an empty shell.

When Dickie's boiler car pulled up, I jumped in as fast as I could. "Let's get out of here."

"Where are we going again?"

"The Bricks," I said, slouching down in my seat and closing my eyes against the memories creeping in. "A weird, low-tech compound ... here, I'll show you."

I gave him the coordinates from my trip with Constance.

"Never heard of it." He shrugged and punched them in. "You don't look so good."

"I'll be okay," I said. "I just have to get the smell of gin and vomit out of my nostrils. I'm having flashbacks to my misspent youth."

"You mean, like two weeks ago?"

I massaged the back of my shoulder where the glass dart had stuck me. The nerve jumped and my upgrade twitched. The unfamiliarity of the arm was itself becoming familiar. "It feels like a lifetime."

"So, what's the smoke?" Dickie turned in his seat and crossed his ankle over his knee. He leaned forward eagerly, his brown eyes comically wide. "You any wiser than the last time I picked you up?"

"Wise might be a stretch."

"What do you need me to do?" He rubbed the seam of his tailored pants between his thumb and middle finger. The slick, slightly iridescent fabric made a hissing noise. "I know I didn't rate for much last time ... Hawkins makes me nervous. But I could stick to the shadows, though, be a lookout. Or I could—"

I let him blabber about all the things he could do and watched the lights streak by as we zipped along the grid. I needed to get off this job without doing any damage to Rae's career. How would Flint take the news of Angelica's murder? Or did he already know? There had to be a way to play it so that I could be out of the picture before the HCPD greys started throwing their weight around. What made a man like Flint tick? The man was a tangle of incongruences. A childless father. A broke man with a rich, dead wife. A high-tech R&D hotshot living with the low-tech nutjobs. There was a thread there. I just needed to tug it and see which bits fell apart.

"So what do you think?" Dickie asked.

The boiler car had pulled onto the darkened streets of the concrete village. This time the houses looked less like adobe homes and more like burial mounds, squatting and grey with the gaping black holes of windows like eyeless sockets staring into the night. The car's lights cast dancing shadows between the buildings so that they seemed to loom out in front of us and then slip away to either side where they followed us in the darkness.

"Creepy," Dickie said, his question forgotten.

I said, "Just drop me in front of the old Bell place and then wait for me down at the entrance to the compound. If I'm not back in an hour, call Tom Weiland. He might need help finding the place."

Relief flooded across my friend's features and he surveyed the strange community. Then he turned back to me with his mouth in a hard, tight line. "You sure you want me to do that?"

"By then I'll either be gone or dead," I said. "Someone will have to clean up this little mess of Flint's. Might as well be Weiland."

"Sure, Bubbles," Dickie said. He didn't look happy as we pulled up in front of Flint's Luddite fortress. Dexter Wagner's body had been removed, but the rain couldn't wash away the evidence of his death. The ghost of his blood stained the wet pavement, black on dark grey. The big, metal gate leaned crookedly, the circular E.B. monogram cracked in two with one side opening toward us as if inviting me inside. I opened the beetle-wing door and ducked into the rain.

Dickie said, "Be careful."

I reached inside the car and squeezed his shoulder. I wished I had something to give him besides gratitude. "Thanks, Dick. For everything.

If something happens to me, take care of Mittens, will you?"

"Oh. Um." His eyes bugged out at me and he bit his bottom lip to stop it from trembling. "Maybe Rae? I'm allergic. To nanoparticles. It's a rare—"

I closed shut the door and slipped through the opening in the gate with a smile on my face that made my cheeks ache. It felt like a long time since I'd stretched those muscles. I held it there until it became a leer as I approached the ominous grey building. I clenched my teeth together and climbed the wide, moulded-concrete terrace steps toward the front door. As if to further proclaim the Brick's dedication to backwardness, a pair of torches lit either side of the great, black entryway, burning with chemical blue flames. I pounded on the door with my metal fist. A twinge of satisfaction burned in my belly when I saw the dent I'd left in the smooth, black wood.

The door cracked open, and the glowing barrel of a plasma rifle poked out into the rain to greet me. A voice growled from the other side of the gun from a face I couldn't see. "Beat it, skid. The boss ain't accepting any more visitors."

"Does Libra's top R&D scientist always have heavies guarding his front door?"

"I said drift, if you know what's good for you." The glowing barrel jabbed me in the chest and made a humming noise as the E-mag field began charging up. The noise made the nerves in my left arm burn.

I shifted my weight away from the gun. "I work for the boss."

He grunted. "Appointment only. No exceptions."

"He invited me," I said.

"He didn't say nothing."

"I'm a little late," I said. "You can ask Constance if she's around."

The gun disappeared and the door slammed shut. I put myself on the opposite side from where I'd been standing and pressed my back against the wood. After a minute or two the door cracked open, and the rifle nosed out again.

I kicked the door wide and brought my upgrade up from underneath the gun, grabbed the barrel and twisted. The guy's fingers cracked and he screamed, unable to release the E-mag grip fast enough. The rifle gave a high-pitched whine, and a bright ball burst out of the barrel, past the terrace, and into the rainy sky. After it had discharged, I wrenched it out of his hands, ripped the battery out of the bottom, and clubbed him with the butt. Blood burst from his nose and he fell to his knees with his hands covering his face. The index finger of his right hand bent at an unnatural angle.

More amateurs. Someone was playing a dangerous game without understanding the rules.

I stepped past the injured guard, kicked him out onto the terrace, and slammed the door behind him. Inside, I pulled a heavy bar down to lock the doors in place, grateful for the low-tech security. Darkness swallowed the entryway completely. I blinked to rid myself of the halos left behind by the eerie blue torches outside. They wouldn't go away and I realized there were more torches farther down the corridor, illuminating nothing. Voices carried along the hall toward me, and I crept my way closer to them, straining my ears to make out who might be waiting for me.

Another set of torches illuminated another black door, guardless this time, from behind which the voices emanated. I pressed my ear against the door, but they were too muffled to decipher. It didn't matter anyway. I was going to do what I'd come there to do. So I pushed on the door and it swung inward on well-oiled hinges, without any effort and hardly a sound.

They didn't notice me immediately. Flint hunched over an old-fashioned wooden desk about the size of a short city block. He wore a deep-plum smoking jacket from a century so long forgotten I wondered if he might have invented time travel and forgotten to tell Libra about it. His thin, curved neck swayed slightly and bobbed his spotty, balding pate back and forth in the low, yellow light. Behind Flint, Constance stood like a woman made of stone, her grey hair and hard face barely visible in the shadows. She stared down on the top of his gleaming head while he blinked through his wire-framed glasses at the stunner to his right.

Miss Scarlett Martinez wore a transparent, black evening gown veined with thin, green circuit traces and blinking processor chips which culminated in a river of parallel lines around her belly button and shot straight up between her breasts in an enthusiastic spray of wires that leaped off the dress and burrowed themselves in the flesh of her bare chest. She sat with one leg crossed elegantly over the other, the split hem of her gown parted to reveal a thick bronze thigh and emerald heels long and deadly enough to be classified as weapons in most corporate states.

I stepped into the room and all three faces turned toward me, like puppets tied to the same string. Ironic, given the circumstances. I said, "I guess my invitation got filed in the junk mail."

"Good to see you again, sweetheart." Scarlett gazed over a bare shoulder at me. "It was getting a little dry in here."

"Don't blame me for the company you keep." I grabbed an overstuffed armchair and spun it to face the desk. "Sorry to barge in here and rearrange your furniture, Flint, but I've had a hard day and I need to sit down."

"Well, what do you want?" Flint barked in his raspy bird voice at me. "Some detective you turned out to be. How'd you get in here anyway? Where's Lou? Never mind that. I want some damned answers. I put you on a confidential job and the first thing you do is march up to Miss Martinez and tell her the whole story?"

"It worked, didn't it?"

He stared at me. They all stared. Flint drummed his fingers on the desk hard enough to leave dents. "What do you mean it worked? Nothing worked."

"I happen to like Miss Martinez," I said. "Or, 'that red-headed vetch' as you so eloquently put it before. And I have an idea that she's here to make a little deal with you. A deal you ought to have made before we had the HCPD all riled up over the stiffs we've stacked up. Where's Angelica?"

Flint's fingers stopped and he turned his beady eyes on me. "She's missing," he said. "And you are incompetent."

"I know you've got friends in the highest of low places," I said to Scarlett. "But don't you think this is a little risky? Do you even have a weapon?"

Scarlett's lips, painted a deep, glittering green to match her dress, spread in a wide smile revealing her big white teeth. "I am the weapon."

"You want me to get rid of her, boss?" Constance said from the shadows. I wondered if he ever let her out to play, or if she just stood guard over him like a gargoyle waiting for the bird to slap her with some fecal matter.

"Don't be silly," Flint snapped, and Constance disappeared a little more. "We have to wrap this business up. I want to be rid of you, Marlowe."

"The feeling is mutual," I said. "What do you mean your daughter is missing?"

"I'm paying you good money," he shouted. His long, bony fingers slapped the top of the desk to emphasize all the stacks of cred he was paying me.

"When?" I asked.

Scarlett laughed—a low, sultry sound—and flicked the blood-red waves of her hair over her shoulder. She said, "My question exactly."

Constance's mouth hardened into a crooked line like a fissure in a rock face. A thin veneer of sweat glossed Flint's forehead, and he clenched his fists into tight balls on top of the desk.

"What do you think I mean? My daughter is missing. I should think even an obvious incompetent like you might be able to puzzle out the meaning of that sentence. Nobody knows where she is. I don't know. Miss Martinez doesn't know. She's not in any of the places she usually goes to... to..."

"To spend Mother's money before it rightfully belongs to her?" I offered.

Flint hissed.

I leaned onto the armrest of the overstuffed chair, rubbing my fingers against the velvet brocade surface and marvelling that such a thing had ever been fashionable. "Well, maybe I am incompetent, but I know where she is, so what does that make you?"

Nobody said anything for a moment. Scarlett shifted in her seat, uncrossed and re-crossed her legs so that she was facing me instead of Flint. Constance seemed to stop breathing entirely. Flint bugged his eyes at me. I let them sit on it for a bit.

"What do you mean, you're the weapon?" I asked the girl.

She rang a finger along the plunging necklace of her gown and stroked the wires coming out of her chest. She said, "If I die, you all die."

My heart did a little stop-start. "Did Vector set you up with that rig?"

"Vector paid the bill," she said. "But I have other friends."

"He was looking for you earlier," I said. "Where were you? Or are you telling? The Heights is a lonely place with only the goons to keep you company."

She laughed again. "Tell me something I don't know."

"What have you done to Angelica?" From the other side of the desk, Flint wheezed. The sweat sheen became beads. The colour had drained from his skin, leaving the age spots in stark relief against the pallor.

Scarlett licked her lips and said, "It's no secret. We took a hack to one of Vector's gaming houses. Angelica was feeling sore about the whole thing. You showing up. She kept going on and on about the money and how much she hated Flint. It kind of put a sour taste in my mouth. I love Angelica, I really do, but I don't want her thinking I'm anything like her father. So I told her maybe we should put off the wedding. Get her accounts squared away and safe from prying hands. Then we could get married and maybe I wouldn't ever see a chip off the block. Doesn't matter. I can afford my brother's schooling with what Vector pays me. I'd be happy just knowing Flint didn't have it either. But Angel was hurt. She thought I was looking for an excuse to call everything off. We fought about it. She hit the tables pretty hard. I waited around, hoping she'd come out of it, but she was just digging herself deeper and deeper into her funk. So I called a hack pod and came here, to tell Flint I'd lay off if he made sure Vector's loans were taken care of."

"You and Angel took a hack," I said. "Why didn't she call Constance? I understand that's the usual arrangement."

I looked at Scarlett, but the question wasn't for her. Flint's voice cut through the silence like jagged metal. "Constance was picking me up from Libra. Why does that matter?"

"Well," I said. "Angelica's back at the Heights. I checked in with Hawkins in security. She came back, alone, and she hasn't left."

I watched each of them carefully, as well as I could with only one set of eyes in my head. But nobody moved. They just looked at me.

"Good," the old man said, finally. "I was worried she'd gotten herself into some trouble."

"Well, she's not off drinking and gambling away her fortune if that's what you mean," I said. "Didn't you try calling the Heights? When you were looking for her?"

Constance stepped out of the shadows and nodded curtly. "I did. They said she wasn't there. Maybe someone had paid the answering service to say she was out."

"That wouldn't be necessary," I said. "They'd just ring the room and Angel wouldn't answer, naturally."

Flint blinked at me once. Again. Then he said, "Naturally?"

I stood up from my chair and everyone in the room tensed. I held my hands up and paced in front of Flint's desk, just close enough to make him nervous. "Now hold on. Let's just line everything up before we start pulling on loose strings. Angelica owes Mick Vector a hundred K stack. She doesn't have the money to pay, and Daddy Dearest refuses to do it. But a little birdie by the name of Bobby Mook sings a little song about a girl named Martinez who'd like to get her hooks into Angelica's fortune. Does that sound about right?"

Flint leaned back in the chair, looking small and frail. He nodded, but only slightly.

"I went to ask Mook about the details of this ill-fated romance," I said. "Only I never quite got around to it on account of Mook being dead when I got there. Shot three times in the heart with a small-bore pistol. Don't worry, though, I didn't call the police."

Flint's shoulders trembled a little and his eyes bugged out even farther. "Murdered?"

Constance still hadn't moved a muscle. Scarlett bounced her green-tipped toes up and down and pressed her lips into a thin line hard enough to make the skin around her mouth turn pale.

"Mook's the kind of guy who likes a little blackmail on the side of his bookie biz," I said. "So anyone might have topped him. Nothing necessarily ties him to Mr. Flint's affairs except for the size of the bullets. Those little target-type guns aren't common in the Grit. You have to have a steady hand and be able to get up close and personal. It's the kind of weapon that requires a bit of finesse. A lady's touch, perhaps. And the interesting thing is, there is a lady who favours such a weapon who is tied to this case."

The silence filled the air, thick as smoke and difficult to breathe through.

"But why Mook was shot I don't know. He was not a danger to Miss Martinez or to Mick Vector, as far as I can tell. Miss Martinez wasn't too shy to talk about the eyes she had on Angelica's fortune.

Vector holds much larger debts. So I wondered if maybe Mook knew a little more than he had let on. Maybe Mook had some ideas about Scarlett and Angelica that he needed to get off his chest. But he didn't get the chance. It doesn't hurt my feelings too much. I didn't know him.

"But then I went to talk to Miss Martinez and we had a nice time until Angelica decided to swat me like a fly. I woke up to a headache and an empty flat. I called it bad luck and went home.

"There I found the lovely with the small-bore pistol, she and her handsy half-wit of a brother named Dexter Wagner. I wasn't too fond of old Dex. Even so, I didn't relish watching him bleed out on your driveway earlier this evening, Mr. Flint, when your enthusiastic chauffeur blew his top off with a hand cannon after he tried to stick up your car. The greys do know about this one, as I'm sure you realized when they came to question your staff. They came to talk to me, too, after someone called them up and tried to pin the incident on me. It didn't work, by the way. But that's two killings. Which leaves the third."

Flint had gone as bright grey as the early morning sky. He spread his hands on the desk in front of him and said through thin, bloodless lips. "The third?"

Constance's expression hadn't changed. The girl looked a little pale, but curious, too, perched on the edge of her seat with her bottom half hanging into open air. I charged ahead, if only to keep up my momentum.

"I met Vector at the Heights, waiting for Miss Martinez, who never did show. He had wanted to share his intel on Mook's shooting, though I'd already passed that little tidbit on to her. He wanted her to lay off Angelica for a bit, just until the greys decided what to do about their suspect list. We had a chat. He left me there, just to annoy the nosy security guard, Hawkins. I decided to have a poke around, just for kicks. And that's when I found Angelica."

I reached into my jacket pocked and pulled out the little gun with the pearly handle, and I dropped it into Scarlett's lap. "Another small bore. More common than I'd guessed. Do you recognize this pretty little piece?"

Her voice trembled with her lips and she seemed to push the words out past a blockage in her throat. But her eyes were clear, and they met mine levelly. "It's mine."

"Where do you keep it?"

"In my bedside table," she said. "I don't really know how to use it, but Angelica insisted I have—"

"Is that where you saw it last?"

"Yes," she said. Then, "No. Angelica had taken it out to show to me how to clean it. She'd left it on the mantel in the sitting room."

"So if someone had surprised her," I said. "She might have picked up the gun?"

She nodded with tears in her eyes. "What do you mean, you found her?"

"You know what I mean. Everyone in this room knows what I mean. Angelica is dead. I found her body stuffed in the bedroom closet with a little, red eye opened up in her forehead and this gun beneath the bed, just waiting to be found."

Flint gurgled something in his throat and fell forward on the desk, his bony fingers clawing at the desk. He fixed his beady eyes on Scarlett Martinez and hissed between clenched teeth, "You!"

The girl stroked the gun in her lap gently, almost lovingly, and loosely left her hand on the butt. I watched her thumb slide over the safety catch and heard the soft click. She didn't know much about guns, but she knew that much.

"There's another possibility," I said. "There's the Wagner woman with the dead brother and the little target pistol, who was so insistent that I lay off this case. She could have shot Angelica. I left her and her gun for the HCPD to sort out. I think she might have some interesting stories to tell."

"You talk too much," Scarlett said and lifted the gun a little. "Get to the point."

"It's obvious who didn't kill Angelica," I said. "Let's consider motive and opportunity. Mick Vector didn't do it. He had 100 K resting on her living to see that inheritance. The Wagner woman didn't do it, no matter who hired her. She couldn't have gotten into the Heights to do the job. Miss Martinez stood to gain much more from having Angelica alive, as well. The only person who gains anything by Angelica's death is Mr. Flint."

Constance lunged, suddenly, a living shadow with the cannon up and pointed at my face before I had a chance to blink. Scarlett was almost as fast. The little gun cracked and a little, red mouth opened up on Constance's wrist. She dropped the cannon on Flint's desk and grabbed her arm, falling back against the wall. Flint lurched forward out of his chair, scrambling for Constance's dropped weapon, but I grabbed him by the back of the smoking jacket with my upgrade and yanked him out of the chair.

"You're a quick study," I said to Scarlett. "Cover him while I call a friend."

Scarlett pinned Flint with the pistol, and I dialled Tom Weiland's private number on my tattler. He didn't pick up, but I left him a 'gram showing Flint and Constance with a short message. "Book 'em, Weiland. And lay off."

I bent Flint over his desk and twisted his arm behind his back. Constance whimpered in the corner and Scarlett bent to pick up her gun too.

Scarlett said, "Of course. Constance could get into the apartment without Hawkins batting an eye. But how did she know Angelica was there?"

"She followed you," I said. "She had the car. Flint hasn't been at the office today. I checked on my way over here."

"And what?" Scarlett turned to Constance. "You thought you'd pin it on me by using my gun?"

"She killed Mook too," I said. "Used the small bore because she knew that's what Ms. Wagner preferred. She hired the duo to put a scare into Angelica so that when she got topped it would look like one of Vector's thugs going too far. Shot poor Dex for believability. But I want to know what Mook died for. Why don't you tell me?" I twisted

Flint's arm, and he wailed a high-pitched keening noise, snivelling against the desk.

"You don't understand what it was like," he whimpered. "I married Evangeline so that she could help me fund my research. I landed a big contract with Libra, everything was perfect—"

"The research you stole from my mother, you mean." Scarlett's eyes had hardened into something ugly. But I held up a hand.

Flint went on. "Then she falls in with these New Humanists and the Mezzanine Rose. She decides my work is immoral. The corruption of the human form. She donated her fortune to anti-tech charities, bought this backward hovel and what was left she willed to Angelica on her twenty-first birthday. She wouldn't let me have a single holocred. We fought about it, and I ..."

"And you killed her," I said.

He nodded miserably, not out of guilt but at having been found out. He sniffed and said, "I gave her something we've been sitting on in the lab, a new drug that wouldn't show up in the toxicology reports. It looked like a stroke. Perfect. But it wasn't until after she was dead that I realized how airtight the inheritance contracts were. I wasn't going to see a chip. It all went to Angelica. Unless she, too, died. Then, there was a loophole in the contract in which I could—with the right documents—have the fortune transferred to my name."

"Where did Mook come in?"

Constance spoke up, her voice like a high, thin wire being plucked. "Forgery,"she said. "I'd inquired about hacking biomarkers on financial documents and he connected me to Flint. He wanted in on it, he wanted to help, dug up the info on Martinez and everything. But when your friend at Libra suggested you talk to Mook, he had to go."

I turned to Scarlett, with her hard eyes swimming behind a wall of tears. "You can shoot him," I said. "You have time."

She looked at me and smiled sadly. She lifted the gun. An ammonia smell came off the old man, and the carpet beneath his feet grew darker. She pressed the barrel of the little gun against his temple. She said, "Bang." Then she dropped the gun in her bag and stalked toward the door.

"Be seeing you, Marlowe," she said, and she disappeared into the darkness of the hallway outside.

Chapter Ten

I SAT IN THE middle of my apartment floor sharing noodle bowls with Rae Adesina and Dickie Roh. Rae had made sure I got the fee I'd been promised before the HCPD confiscated Angelica's fortune and passed it off to the family lawyers to fight over. So I'd splurged and invited Dickie and Rae for takeout and a pay-per-play VR gaming experience in my living room via an expensive rented console and visilenses.

"Oo, oo, oo!" Dickie jumped to his feet while browsing the game menu on his headset, somehow managing not to spill his noodle bowl on my head. "This one! It's based on an old Raymond Chandler story called Trouble is My Business about an Old Earth private eye back in the early 20th century!"

I rolled my eyes, even though he couldn't see me. "I think I've had enough of that in real life."

Rae pushed the biofoam container away and wiped her electric blue lips with a napkin. Somehow, it didn't budge. Her black skin shimmered with some kind of internal light that my brain couldn't make sense of. I'd asked. She claimed it was proper hydration, nutrition, and plenty of rest, but I didn't buy it. Must be some kind of gene-therapy.

She said, "So, I got the promotion."

"Congratulations!" I slurped a noodle and clicked my chopsticks together like tiny clapping hands. "Does that mean you can score me a better upgrade?"

"Not until you start taking care of that one." Rae arched a thin black eyebrow at me over the frames of her glasses. "Where's that SmartPet of yours? I'm going to program it to remind you of your maintenance schedule."

"Hey, Mittens," I shouted. "Quit hiding out in the bedroom and come be sociable."

"I'm a cat."

I put my noodle bowl down and rubbed my hands together gleefully. "Come on, come out and show Rae and Dickie the present I got for you."

Dickie took the headset off and called out, "Here kitty, kitty!"

"Perhaps you should explain to this imbecile what happened the last time there was an invited guest in this apartment."

"Come out, Mittens," I said. "That's an official command."

There was some muffled cursing from the bedroom and then a simulated click, click, click of the SmartPet walking down the hall. The cat emerged with a look of pure hatred in its narrowed yellow eyes where it glared at me over a cartoon pig nose. Little pink triangular ears twitched with rage, and a curly cue tail attempted to swish back and forth but only bounced up and down.

Dickie snorted, then gasped. "Oh no, I think I got a noodle up my nose!"

Rae tipped her oblong blue afro back and cackled. "What have you done to it? Why would you be so cruel?"

"After all I did for you." Mittens hissed. Through the costume skin, it came out more like a snuffle.

"Yeah, you've been swell," I said. "Right up to the part where you told Weiland how desperately lonely I am, and that if he had ever cared about me, he should probably check in every once in a while."

"Well, it's true." The cat stomped its foot, and a little boot shaped like a pig's hoof clicked against the floor. "And I can't help it. It's part of my programming. He's registered as a safe contact, and you do miss him, whether you want to admit it or not."

"I forgive you," I said. "And after a week of piggy penance you can go back to being your usual delightful self."

"I'm going to go do some updates," the cat grumbled and clip-clopped back into the bedroom.

Dickie and Rae watched me carefully after the cat disappeared. Then Rae said, "So you forgive the pet, but are you ready to forgive Tom?"

I balled up my napkin in my fist and tossed it into my bowl. "Not even close."

"He did ride in all guns blazing and save you from the Bricks," Dickie said.

"Sure, after I'd already incapacitated the bad guys and started his paperwork for him."

"But he left you out of the statements?" Rae's voice tightened. "I don't think I can handle any more 'accidents' happening to my friends."

"Yeah," I said. "He did. I can go back to lying low. No offence, Rae, but I don't think I'll be doing any more favours for friends."

"Sorry it turned out like that," Rae said. "I really did think it would be an easy job."

Dickie finished his noodles and scooped up the rest of the garbage. "I'll clean up. You set the game up. Please, just nothing where I have to run around in a half-naked superhero outfit. I always feel so depressed after logging out of one of those games."

My tattler pinged and a 'gram of Tom Weiland's face hovered above my wrist. I groaned. "It begins."

Rae stood up. "I've got to visit the girls' room." She tiptoed into the hallway.

I ran a hand through my hair and answered the call before nerves or pent-up anger could get the better of me. I said, "Just because a robot cat tells you it's okay to call—"

"Bubbles, listen to me." Tom's grey eyes were pinched at the corner and the bags beneath them were even darker than they were the last time we spoke. "Harold squealed about you to Swain. Told him you had connections with some gambling king pin and were poisoning the Grit against him."

"What? That's not true. I'm staying as far away from Swain as I can."

"I tried to tell him that." Tom rubbed a big hand over his face and looked at the wall behind my head. He said, "Swain's livid, though. And paranoid. You've got to do better than lie low, Bubs. You've got to get out of town."

"What do you mean 'get out of town?' Where the hell am I going to go?"

"Scatter," he said. "Now."

Dickie and Rae peered into the living room with wide eyes. Sweat had broken out on Tom's forehead.

"He's gunning for you, Bubbles," he said, and his voice shook. "On both sides of the law."

He killed the transmission, and the silence that hung in the room after his voice was thick enough to suffocate.

"Sorry guys," I said. "Party's over. Looks like I'm on the lam."

THE END

Glossary

THE FOLLOWING ARE SOME of the slang words I've used in HoloCity Case Files and Bubbles in Space. Where applicable, I have indicated the original meanings of these words from classic pulp novels. Did I miss any? Please let me know if you'd like a term added to the list! Send me a message at contact@scjensen.com.

Bangtail – space shuttles, originally "racehorse"
Boiler – both personal and rental maglev vehicles, originally "car"
Cush – money (a cushion, something to fall back on), original meaning
Dizzy – crazy or foolish, originally "to be gaga for"
Drift – get lost, original meaning
Fade – to kill, originally "go away" or "get lost"
Feedcasters – live video jockeys on social media
Feedreels – live video footage covering news, social events, gossip, and entertainment topics
Glow-up – originally "a glow" was to be drunk, here used as a drug-induced high

'Gram – hologram image or video

Grid – the electromagnetic transportation grid

Hack – a taxi, original meaning

Highbinder – a corrupt official, original meaning

Kiss – to punch, original meaning

Kretek – clove cigarettes, original meaning

Long bird – sky train

Pinch – a drug addict, originally "to arrest"

Pro skirt – a prostitute, original meaning

Rate – used to indicate veracity or quality. "That rates" may mean either "That's good" or "That sounds true," originally "to be good" or "to count for something"

Scatter – a hideout, or to hide, original meaning

Shill – an accomplice of a hawker, gambler, or swindler who acts as an enthusiastic customer to entice or encourage others, original meaning

Silk – good/okay, original meaning

Skin – a nanoparticle "shell" used to change ones appearance, often used for robots, androids, and personal enhancement for those who can afford it

Slug – subway

Tattler – a communication device similar to a smartphone

Ticket – a license, original meaning

Topped – killed, original meaning

Twist – a romantic partner, original meaning (female only)

Upgrade – a cybernetic replacement part

Vetch – derogatory term for females and femmes

Author's Note

THANK YOU FOR READING Dames for Hire! This tale was born out of my love for the classic noir pulp novels of Raymond Chandler and Dashiell Hammett, and the 1980s cyberpunk movement in science fiction. I love the tropes in these genres and I've tried to incorporate as many as I could.

One trope I've flipped in this story, though, is that of the alcoholic detective. Bubbles is a milestone character for me because she is the first character I've written who reflects my own battles with alcohol abuse and (thankfully) my recovery. I hope she will provide both insight and inspiration to others in their journeys toward sobriety. We need more sober heroes!

I will be releasing many more novella length stories in the HoloCity Case Files series in the coming years. The first arc of the Bubbles in Space series is now complete and ready to binge. If you'd like to be one of the first to read the next instalment in either series (or future side series), please join my VIP readers club where you will be notified of pre-orders, new releases, and you can sign up to be on my Advanced Review Copy team!

You can join via the pop-up on my website, www.scjensen.com, or by clicking this link.

If you enjoyed Dames for Hire, please consider leaving a review on Amazon and Goodreads. Reviews help authors improve their craft and help readers find the right books for them.

Thanks for your support!

Also By S.C. Jensen

Bubbles in Space

#1 Tropical Punch
#2 Chew 'Em Up
#3 Pop 'Em One
#4 Spit 'Em Out
#5 Cherry Bomb

HoloCity Case Files

Dames for Hire
HoloCity Hard Boys
Neon Goldfish

Undercity

(coming Spring 2022)
Rebellion – Timekeepers' War Book 1

Resistance – Timekeepers' War Book 2
Revolution – Timekeepers' War Book 3

Join Bubbles Marlowe on her first detective cases in...

HoloCity Case Files

A series of standalone cyber-noir mystery novellas inspired by
Raymond Chandler's 'Philip Marlowe' short stories.

Complete Series now available!

Bubbles in Space is
"...gritty and glamorous, violent and dazzling..."